MESSAGE TO JENNY

There is something missing. Where is the dead woman's entitlements card? It has no use to a killer. As soon as she was scanned at the scene, her idents and access to all she had, ceased to exist.

"Pull Wilkerson, Folcoup homicide files—personal effects, please."

The deskcomp begins working. It places the two lists side by side on my wall.

Could it be that the killer takes a souvenir? The thought gives me pause, makes me leave the desk and stare out the window at the yellow haze.

Trophy? Souvenir? The answer makes my skin crawl. The messages to me in the corpses' thoughts. The placement of one of them in an ice-house. Entitlements cards. This isn't about "stop me before I kill again." No.

How else will the killer prove his identity to me when the mystery is unraveled?

He wants me to find him.

CIRCLE OF ONE

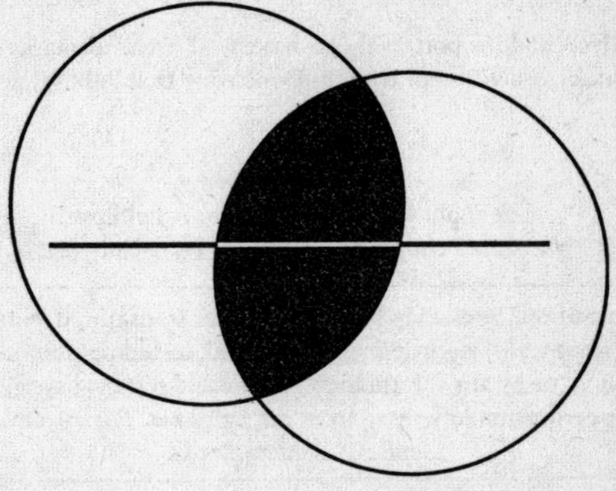

ERIC JAMES FULLILOVE

BANTAM BOOKS
NEW YORK • TORONTO • LONDON • SYDNEY • AUCKLAND

CIRCLE OF ONE
A Bantam Spectra Book/November 1996

ISBN-0-553-57575-9
Published simultaneously in the United States and Canada

Bantam Books are published by Bantam Books, a division of Bantam Doubleday Dell Publishing Group, Inc. Its trademark, consisting of the words "Bantam Books" and the portrayal of a rooster, is Registered in U.S. Patent and Trademark Office and in other countries. Marca Registrada. Bantam Books, 1540 Broadway, New York, New York 10036.

PRINTED IN THE UNITED STATES OF AMERICA

OPM 10 9 8 7 6 5 4 3 2 1

To Brian and Michael
the best sons
a man could ask for.

PROLOGUE

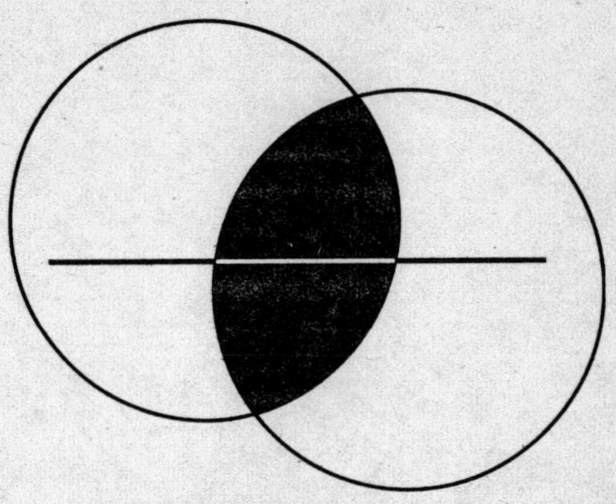

Los Angeles, California—May, 2040

The soundless lift opened after rising three hundred stories onto seven thousand square feet of pleasure palace; they called it Heaven. Bilious clouds moved across a ceiling dome of clearest blue even though it was darkest night.

"I'd die for *you*!" the naked hologram gushed as her tears flowed down between impossibly fulsome breasts. Felonious quantities of drugs were being consumed even though he, Derrick Trent, was a cop. As if this crowd gave a damn—sex that would stop clocks, wallets that would kill, the messy real world mercifully concealed hundreds of millibars of pressure below them. The glitterati, the power players, moved from room to room and back to the cavernous sunken living room with its strobes and groping and music. Muscle men in G-strings struggled to thrust fluted champagne glasses into all the hands that wanted it.

The matron, Demarche, greeted them at the elevator. Old, grey, shrewd, and rich. Half of the population in

LA that mattered fit that description, with or without the gold lamé muumuu.

"And welcome to my world," Demarche said, offering each passenger a platinum-plated inhalator of Stim and a headset. One of the perks of being up for a detective's shield, Trent thought as he refused and considered himself fortunate to be under Demarche's digitized illusion of clear weather.

He caught sight of an LAPD captain going into one of the back rooms with a brunette looker. The captain was the unofficial reason he was here.

"You've heard of the place. Take a look," the section chief had said when he came on shift. He was one of the boys. He was going places. This was his first taste of the good life, a gold shield that was his if he proved adept at knowing when to look the other way.

So, go fetch the captain before his heart gives out. Try CPR if you're too late.

Otherwise, practice not noticing things, wink, wink.

<status check?> he whispered in his head. The tiny computer buried under his hairline whisked his thoughts into the secured communications network.

<nothin' to worry about,> the dispatcher whispered back. Trent flicked his hand at his hairline to make sure that his collar was turned up. Didn't want people to see that the tiny sockets at the base of his neck were plugged in, didn't want people to think that he was noticing things.

Somebody, female, pushed up against him briefly and palmed his crotch, tugged him to the center of the dance floor, and someone tried to push an inhalator in his nose. He turned away, coming face-to-face with the hologram that said "I'd die for *you*!" and spread her arms wide. The afterlife beckons, Derrick Trent thought with a wicked smile.

Demarche swept into one of the back rooms, her grey eyes glittering. The fifteen women milling around the sumptuous banquet gradually stopped chattering, although Chloe stuffed one last jumbo shrimp into her mouth. She didn't mind Chloe's indulgence. After all, these were her special girls.

<200 paying guests so far, 15 comp'd.> her support staff whispered into her head. "Ladies. A few words, please?" Blonde, brunette, redhead, it didn't matter. She looked at them and saw the color of money, potential to be unleashed. *<what about the ancillaries?>*

"I want to remind you why you're here," Demarche said softly. She looked each girl in the eye.

"You must smile at the men, smile and talk to them and be interested in them. Sex they can get cheaper, better, get it jacked into their heads a million ways. There are others here for that. *You* have to make them want *you*." She surveyed the room. *<don't have the ancillaries yet. prelims look good. lotta credits out there tonight.>*

"And the women?" Jenny asked, because Jenny was new.

Demarche smiled coldly. "The women always come with men they are interested in. You are their transport to fulfillment. They may be jealous, they may be bored. But they will all be wealthy. That should always govern your response." *<matilda and eduardo arrive yet?>*

Jenny looked, a question on her face.

<negatory> "Of course"—Demarche laughed slightly—"you can always ply your talents elsewhere

should you not become, ah, accustomed to the house rules."

Oh, no, the group said en masse, Demarche noted with satisfaction. Heaven was the place to be if you qualified. These women arrived with too many horror stories about freelancing; too many of them ended up dead or broken in the real world. Always a pity, given their unique talents. Their capabilities. "Line up, girls. Let me look at you before we go into battle."

A nervous giggle from fifteen pairs of perfectly rouged lips. She was efficient but thorough in her inspection, telling one to adjust her makeup, another to change her attitude. Another to make sure that she wasn't plugged in: she rearranged the girl's hair to cover the neck sockets.

And then there was the new girl, Jenny. Demarche regarded her critically. She was beautiful, tall at five nine with a cascade of blond hair and green eyes, a *Cosmopolitan* body. Precisely the type to be most fragile once they were pressed to maximize their extraordinary capabilities.

"Very nice." Demarche ran her hand down the translucent silk of the girl's blouse, her fingernails just brushing the firm flesh of Jenny's breast.

Jenny blushed. "Thank you."

"I have a special assignment for you tonight, dear. You have piggybacked quite a bit, hmm? You did not deceive an old woman in our interview?"

"You tested me. You checked my references."

"Umm-hmm." Demarche pulled her close, feeling the smooth skin beneath the silk.

"Fifty thousand," Demarche whispered. "A special, special order. Just for you."

Jenny pulled away. "Fifty?" The glint in her eyes was as Demarche expected.

The old matron smiled and nodded. "A generous cut of the total fee, of course."

"Which is what, if I may ask?"

Demarche shook her head, still smiling. "You may not ask. Ever." She stared into Jenny's eyes, pressing her point without words, without threat. The other girls were milling around the still closed doors to the living room, eyeing the two of them jealously. Jenny glanced their way and saw Chloe, nervous, pumped up, the scent of burnout around her like a shroud. Jenny looked back at Demarche and into the steely grey of her lively cold eyes, noting the bemused arch of her left eyebrow. Girls had been known to disappear from Heaven, some even to take a three-hundred-story express straight to hell.

Jenny nodded, accepting that she'd been outflanked by the ruthless old bitch. Business is business.

<got the numbers. you're looking at a cool half mill in ancillaries right now.> "Good," Demarche said as much to the voice in her head as to Jenny. "Ladies? Tonight is a masked ball. Adds to the fun, don't you think?"

They agreed in a cascade of nervous chatter.

"Stay close to me," Demarche told Jenny as she threw the doors open wide.

Derrick found himself spilled to the edge of the living room listening to some old standard pumped up with a techno beat. Demarche emerged with fifteen of the most beautiful women on the planet, high-stepping, he imagined, to the thumping bass.

He gawked at their physical, unattainable beauty,

felt acutely his limitations in the face of pretty that only money can buy.

Oh, to be rich . . . And then he saw her. Blond, green eyes. Tall, gorgeous. Through the microprocessor in his head he asked dispatch

<the list of women in Demarche's stable. got a blonde, five feet nine?>

<checking.> She was demurely tagging along behind Demarche. Where does she find these women?

He watched as men approached her and were quietly rebuffed. Not your normal whore, then. A piggybacker, perhaps?

<nothing on a blonde with that description. must be new.> She stared at the ceiling with its fake sky, eyes clear, not on anything and Derrick Trent felt part of himself falling away, stripped away like burning skin . . .

. . . and he knew in an instant that he wanted her, at any price. Derrick Trent made his way through the crowd to where she was standing.

Another saw Jenny at the same time. He was wearing a costume mask and had been properly invited to Demarche's ridiculous showcase. Unlike Derrick Trent, he could afford the twenty-thousand-credit entry fee.

As if money alone can make any of these people special.

He studied her, watching calmly as Demarche fawned over this one or that. His mind automatically reached out to her, but curiously, he stopped himself.

Not yet. In that instant of awareness he'd seen exactly what Demarche had in mind for Jenny.

That was her name. Jenny. A piggybacker. A

telepath/capable like he, except on a much smaller scale. He smoothed back his black hair and adjusted his mask. He had a feeling, a strong feeling, that this Jenny was special. It would not do for Demarche to fawn over him, for him to meet her on the proprietress's terms.

There would be time later. *After.* He closed his eyes. Felt her beauty, her edge, possession life or death. Love her, want her, need her, all of it a cascade triggered by something in her thoughts, something so deep that he was afraid of the connection.

Maybe Heaven has given me a miracle after all. And he felt the raw energy of his mind surge and seethe, felt the need to calm his fears.

He reached out with the power of his thoughts alone and drew a woman to him, one selected at random from a sea of sinful possibilities. Her name, he saw, was Elizabeth. He flicked a glance over her shoulder at Jenny, smiled, and grasped Elizabeth's consciousness like it was a lump of coal he could hold in his hand. He grasped her puny intellect and squeezed it just a little, then released it. He gazed into her eyes, saw what he wanted to see in her mind. Saw what he'd planted there, just for fun . . .

take the next man i meet in my mouth,
in my mouth . . .

He sent her away and slid quietly to another corner of the huge room.

"Oh, Senator, that would be quite apropos!" Demarche was saying as Derrick Trent slid into earshot. Out of the corner of her eye the matron saw the policeman and thought initially that he was a gate crasher, but her support staff identified him and his association to the LAPD captain who had, at last count, worn out three of the lesser lights Demarche kept around for straight sex. He waited patiently at the edge of Demarche's space as Demarche ignored him and greeted others more worthy of cultivation.

He isn't interested in me at all, she thought after a few moments. Part of her watched as Trent observed the senator taking a transdermal of Stim; the damned flatfoot was plugged in and could very well be recording the whole scene for posterity and the future benefit of his bank account. She turned to Jenny, nodding at Trent.

"You have an admirer."

Jenny shrugged. "Losers don't admire me."

"Take him away from me, please. Ditch him and hurry back."

Jenny frowned and grabbed a startled Derrick.

"You. Dance. Now."

And she led him away.

He wasn't bad-looking but he couldn't dance a lick. Could stand to lose a good twenty pounds or so, maybe cut back on the donuts in the squad mobile . . .

"So what's your name?" he shouted at her.

. . . And he has absolutely no rap whatsoever. She ignored his question, preferring the din of music being pumped into the room.

He moved closer, a hazard to navigation, and put his hand on her shoulder.

"I said, what's your name?"

She flicked his hand away. "It isn't 'Fondle Me Here,' pal."

He looked at her, irritated and fascinated at the same time. "You're pretty."

"No shit. And you are a cop."

"I thought you might like men with guns. For protection, you understand."

Get real! "So what do we need protecting from tonight?"

"Nothing. Favor to a superior officer. Looks good on the stat sheet."

He's staring at my breasts, she thought. She turned her back.

He tapped on her shoulder. Reluctantly she turned back to face him.

"I take it you work here."

"You might say that. You might say that I'm working overtime right now."

"You like it? Here, I mean."

Another slob who wants to rescue me . . .

"It pays the bills."

She looked into his eyes then, warning him away.

"Jenny." Demarche, behind her. Time to cash in her chips.

"See ya, cowboy," she said over her shoulder to Trent.

Demarche led her back to one of the more private suites off the main hall. The music was reduced to a dull throb as they crossed the threshold and then absorbed to nothing as Demarche closed the soundproofed door. The claustrophobic isolation gave Jenny her first wave of jitters that always came before a session.

Demarche turned up the lights.

She took it all in, the standard piggybacker setup. Two low flat couches with supple cushions, a buffet of drugs laid carefully out on a silver tray. A wafer-thin device with twin displays, oscilloscopes Jenny liked to call them, with headbands for her and the object of the session. A neural interface.

Demarche standing by the closed door.

"Take off your clothes, please."

Definitely not standard. Not standard at all. Piggybacker clients wanted out-of-body thrills for a fee. They hooked into her mind via the interface, shared space in her head, real time. And they always wanted Jenny because she was beautiful . . .

"Why?". . . beautiful, and accessible the way only a piggybacker could be accessible even though she didn't do "it."

"In thirty seconds fifty thousand credits is going to walk into this room. If you are not what they want, then fifty thousand credits will walk out." Demarche smiled coldly. "Let's make a good first impression, shall we?"

She waited, Jenny hesitated. "Do you think people come here for ordinary thrills, girl?"

Ten times the fee. A million times the action. Was it worth it? Jenny had always been the best. People wanted the intimacy of being in her head, of thinking nasty thoughts while measuring her feelings from the inside. The legacy of her capabilities, the filthy residue they left behind in her, indelible stains of dark fantasy and wild emotion that couldn't be washed away like semen from an unwanted lover. All endured for a price. *But never this much . . .*

Demarche looked at her watch. She motioned toward the silver tray. "Something to relax, perhaps?"

Jenny shook her head, no. Dope and piggybacking don't mix.

A knock on the door, soft yet insistent.

You sought Demarche because she could protect you. Spread your legs and do "it." That's the price of protection.

Remember your last freelance assignment? Jerkoff wanted to touch a woman from the inside, that's what he'd said.

Surprise! During the piggyback he pulled a pistol with one bullet, made her hands spin the cylinder, made her put his gun to *her* head so that he could experience *her* fear, a woman's fear, a woman's hatred of guns. *From the inside.*

Made her pull the trigger. *Click! Are you afraid, bitch?*

Second time. *Click. Yeah, you're sick with it. Sick and afraid, piss your pants afraid.*

Third time. Funniest feeling, there on the edge. Like she could destroy him somehow even as she felt her finger tighten on the trigger again, as she came closer and closer to destroying herself.

Even as she knew that the bullet was waiting for the hammer to fall if she pulled the trigger a fourth time.

Demarche glared at Jenny. <tell chloe to come to room seven right now.> No chances, always a backup plan with the new ones.

Fifty thousand credits. Jenny swiftly undid her blouse, slid her skirt down over her ankles. Removed her panties.

Demarche opened the door. "Matilda! Oh, and this must be Eduardo, yes!"

They crowded into the room as Demarche dimmed the lights. Matilda, Jenny could see, was ancient, at least seventy, with skin pulled so tight from face lifts that she looked like a jeweled gargoyle. Matilda and Demarche bussed cheeks, Matilda lowering her black eye mask so that it wouldn't get in the way.

Eduardo was a massive man, six feet two easily, sculpted muscles, and absurdly good-looking. An old crone and her boy toy, and Jenny began to get a bad feeling about things.

"And this is Jenny," Demarche gushed, and in her head turned up the track lighting where Jenny was standing, just a teensy bit.

Eduardo grinned as Matilda circled her, brushing Jenny's bare shoulders with her razor-sharp nails.

"Demarche," she said as she finished inspecting the goods, "you've outdone yourself. Hasn't she, Eduardo?"

Eduardo pulled at the Velcro strip on his very tight pants. He was large, fully erect. Matilda caressed his organ with her palsied hand.

"Hmm. Very nice. She'll do, Demarche. She'll do."

<cancel chloe she can go back to the party> Demarche thought, and the wireless net whispered her command.

Now isn't this some sick shit. Matilda led Eduardo over to Jenny by his cock, motioning her to spread her legs a bit so she could rub the head of his penis against her blond bush.

"Shall we begin?" Matilda asked. Demarche looked

at Jenny. *Last chance,* the look said. *You know what's coming.* She'd asked herself a million times before coming to Demarche: how bad could "it" be?

Bad, Jen. Bad as a fourth pull on the trigger. That's the price of protection.

"He's had all his shots, I hope." A feeble entreaty. Matilda laughed. "This is Heaven, dear. You want risk, go to South Centro."

Jenny, resigned, sat down on one of the couches. Demarche paused at the door on her way out. "If there's anything else you need, ask," Demarche said, and withdrew.

Matilda lay down on the other couch and snugged a headband to her temple. Jenny took the other in her hand as she waited for the equipment to cycle. Eduardo, big as all outdoors, began taking off his shirt, his eyes holding Jenny's.

Jenny lay down. She was strong for a piggybacker, but like all piggybackers needed the neural interface to effect the transfer and boost her native telepathic abilities. It wasn't at all like swapping out personalities embedded on a computer chip.

It was better. Much better than that.

She closed her eyes against Eduardo's looming form, against the sudden bile in her throat, waiting for the phase shift—

. . . *of entry* . . . she caught her breath at the whispered rush of the old crone's consciousness merging with her own, Matilda's thoughts as dry as tumbleweed in her head. Jenny looked across at the other couch, at Matilda's withered body, empty now of everything except basic autonomous body functions.

Matilda laughed inside her head.

To be young again, Matilda thought, *'tis priceless!* and Jenny felt her hands moving down the scale of her body past her breasts to her upper thighs.

I need to explore this body, child.

Eduardo bent over to kiss her lips, kissed them and moved his tongue down her neck as Matilda cried out in ecstasy in Jenny's head, the effect electric . . .

Eduardo pressed a finger between her legs to see if she was ready in some parody of passion.

She was not.

He began to lap at her as Matilda squealed, forcing Jenny to respond with silken wetness, her legs opening wide for Eduardo, Matilda screaming *fuck me fuck me fuck me,* Eduardo lowering himself onto her . . .

Revulsion—the bad thing back in her head, the scent of another in her nostrils as Jenny began to withdraw into a corner of her mind. Longer hair, whippet-thin body, less mass, less manners, intent as clear as a bell in his head, Eduardo's hot breath on her neck as he pressed against her with his weight and muscle—

worth it, worth it to be young again, Matilda thought as she tried to pull Jenny's knees to her chest—

i bought you, bitch, spread your legs . . .

Resistance. *The bad thing.*

i bought you! The bad thing stronger, the fear, *stronger*. Insatiable.

. . . a subtle thing, a line crossed, a dry twig, something snapping in her, shaking her senses. Instinct as Jenny began to seize control, pushing Eduardo back from the brink of entering her, fighting his lean mass, rolling from the couch to avoid him. Instinct and preservation of something greater than self . . .

you're mine! i own you! the thoughts flashing

through her, the anger. Jenny reached out to the interface, fighting the resistance in her body, her own muscles rebelling—

don't do it, i want him, DON'T

and then Matilda's voice receding with hollow echo as Jenny reset the interface, draining Matilda from her head . . .

A knee to Eduardo's groin as she grabbed her clothes. Eduardo tearing at her blouse.

Matilda stirring in her own body, hands clutching at withered thighs, pulling her knees to her chest, moaning for Eduardo . . .

Jenny stumbling out of the room.

He saw her as she pulsed into the living room like she'd been popped out of a miniature cannon. He saw her and smiled behind his mask. Her blouse was torn and showing a hint of the soft flesh beneath as he opened his mind to her thoughts, straining to hear her inside voice in a room crowded with extraneous thoughts. And suddenly, there she was. In an instant he had confirmation of all of her secrets as they oozed out from under her defenses, her utterly futile defenses. He lost himself, too, just because of who she was. Just because of what she was. Utterly lost himself. A frightening thing.

A *bad thing, too.*

Commotion behind her. An old woman jabbing angrily at Demarche, the matron coolly surveying the crowd. He reached out for the pair, found their thoughts like a single piece of straw in a haystack, and understood completely. Jenny moved into the dancing on the living-room floor, wishing to hide.

He positioned himself just so, willing her to come to him.

She waded into the dancing crowd, thinking about the best way to leave, Demarche probably looking for her right now somewhere behind her.

She bumped into the masked man who took her hands and pulled her close. She thought it was the stupid cop from before; the build was similar but the mask obscured the face. Something about him . . .

For a brief second she felt safe, dancing in his arms, the embrace close, real, unlike . . .

. . . Eduardo.

She pulled back to put distance between their bodies. She could hear Matilda screaming over the din of the party, over the music in her head. Demarche . . . Demarche . . .

Fifty thousand was both too much and not enough, a terrible mistake, a fatal mistake.

And Demarche's cut? Twice as much? Five times? How much anger would her failure purchase? Jenny trembled at the thought.

"You have to get me out of here, cowboy," she whispered to her dance partner.

"Not yet."

"You don't understand . . ." Demarche's voice raised, angry, behind her.

"We haven't gotten to know each other yet, Jenny. You're going to need me as much as I need you."

Save me . . . "I need you to get me out of here!"

Demarche pushing through the crowd, walking through the hologram.

"You're already in Heaven, Jenny. Relax and enjoy it."

Demarche's hand on her shoulder, pulling her around, the blow to her face accomplished before Jenny could think about reacting.

"You're through, you little bitch."

Another slap, this one loud enough to evacuate the dance floor and send Jenny to one knee with the coppery taste of blood in her mouth.

The masked man standing calmly above her, Demarche raising her leg, the short spiked heel gleaming in the strobes.

You're pretty, the masked man said. In her head, without words, a scythe through the music. Demarche stamping down with the spike, just missing her hand and gouging a run in the expensive carpet.

Yeah. Pretty . . . and he let the power surge into her, taking her supple mind and wrenching it . . .

Jenny blinked, and Demarche ground her heel into the palm of her hand, tearing Jenny's flesh . . .

The voice blasting into her head, pain terrific pain as something *twisted* and tore free, peeling back something tangible, a barrier between forever and the rising wail of voices in her head.

Whoa! Next thing you know Demarche will have mud wrestling . . . and Jenny could tell that this thought came from a fat man in a monothread business suit three-people deep in the crowd.

She was hearing thoughts . . . but she wasn't powerful

enough to interface with thin air, the pain, the voices a babble of confusion . . .

Wonder if I can get the redhead to suck my . . . Wealthy businessman, some distance from the action, voices cascading over Jenny's physical pain, the telepathic links opening wide, wider than ever . . . her blood sinking in, lost in the maroon carpet . . .

. . . and then something strong, augmented, amplified in some way—

take the next man i meet in my mouth . . .

And Demarche:

Cunt! Kill her!

Demarche's anger a thunderclap in Jenny's head, a picture of the next blow as clear as the signal from Demarche's brain to her fist . . .

Derrick Trent stepping in between them, absorbing the punch, restraining Demarche, his voice in Jenny's head

protect her

and in the fading distance a chuckle and words of chilling certainty:

We'll meet again, Jenny. I'll be around.

BOOK ONE

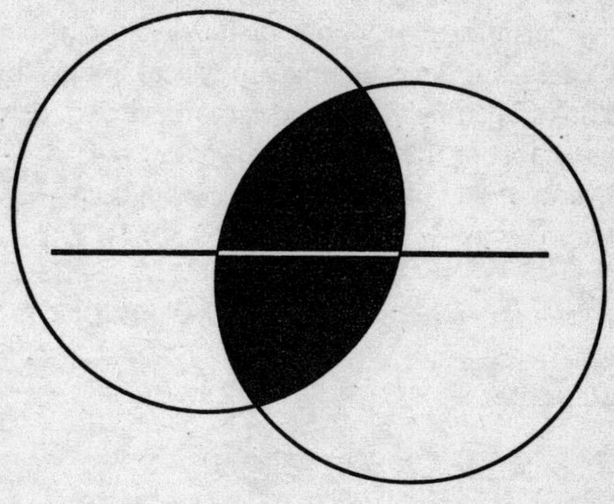

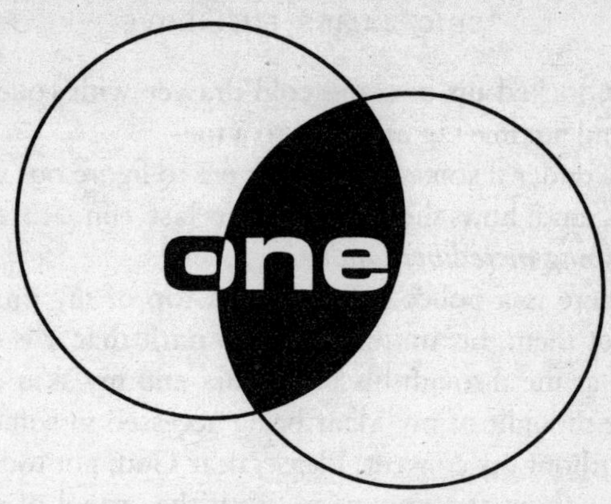

Los Angeles, California—March, 2050

There's something incredibly fatalistic about running away. The furtive backward glance, the note, the resignation, the ending of one life and the beginning of another, another inevitably diminished because we are older than before and, like animals, constantly dying inside.

I cannot run. The great wave of thinking man washes over me every day, the love, the hatred, the lies, death like the occasional boom of distant thunder that lets you know that it's raining somewhere. Trapped like a butterfly on a pin, I twist under the impact of their hot sweaty breath, their thoughts, all of them, all around me *all the time.*

Welcome to my world. Los Angeles, Hollywood Boulevard, the discards, the hopeful, the hopeless. Give it time and they are all variations on the same theme somewhere out on the curve of human existence. Although I only pass through, I hear them the way they hear themselves because I am never alone. I wonder which one of them will end up on the County slab today, locked up in some cold drawer with rollers for feet and a name tag attached to a toe.

I wonder if someone will ask me to figure out where, when, and how they made their last run . . . *there's something incredibly fatalistic . . .*

There is a police helicopter on top of my building. One of them, his uniform blue so dark that it is black, looks at me through his binoculars and my skin crawls at the thought of my ident being accessed in some base net without my consent. Please, dear God, not today.

. . . about running away. With the crowd of execu-types. Into the building. Thoughts of morning coffee and the crush of business, of lovers and wives, of dark and evil things that lurk just beneath the surface.

I heard the whine of the starter from the roof as I walked in. It takes a deep breath to calm my nerves, which are not calmed because I don't believe in coincidence. The elevator chimes, and my floor, mauve carpet and locked oaken doors—a thin veneer for the stout security metal beneath—and I swipe the card through the reader.

I look at Didi, my expression clear. Don't fuck with me. Just give it to me straight.

She does, too. Hands me my headset. "LAPD has a wet one for you." She hands me my gun, an ancient pistol that is well oiled and cared for.

"The LZ is hot, Jen."

Dammit, Deeds, why couldn't you lie for once? A bad day, a bad day. "Where?"

"South Central. Icehouse. Sniper fire reported."

Headset, weapon, ammunition. I buckled them on, careful to opaque my skirt.

"Better hurry." The advice is redundant. "Clock's running on this one."

"How long have they been up there?"

"Ten minutes, easy."

Shit.

The heels go under Didi's desk, a pair of flats slip on. Headset, weapon, ammunition. Out the door, bounding up the stairs to the roof, the other direction so appealing it hurts to think about the steps leading down.

"Deeds, can you hear me?" The boom mike has been acting up lately. There's no wireless in South Centro . . .

She whispers in my ear, a calm yes that is drowned out by the thumping rotor blades.

The officers are already aboard and the pilot is barely keeping the thing on the roof.

The clock is running.

Dear God, another one.

"Who?" I shout over the noise. That slight vertigo as the pilot pivots and pulls away in a hurry.

"Riva Barnes. Secretary to Arnold Waters."

"Arnold who?" The chopper is a French make, fast and sleek. I hate the things, the speed and the black paint and the pilots who wish they could fly jets and lose themselves in that fantasy way below the speed of sound.

"Waters. Big-time industrialist."

"What the hell's his secretary doing in South Central?"

"Getting whacked. By whom, that's what we want you for, sweetness."

"Cut the crap, Derrick." Derrick Trent, LAPD. We go back a long way.

We cut through the smog at a good clip, the city a bowl filled with smoke all around us. The break in the hydrocarbon clouds reveals the change as we pass into no-man's-land, South Centro. The dead zone for the normals who don't happen to be privileged, and by definition there are a shitload of them.

The chopper banks low, avoiding the updraft from a burning car. Kids below scatter like bugs when the light turns on, expecting steel-jacketed slugs. But we aren't here to play with the locals.

There are other helicopters around, big gunships pumping tracers into targets on the ground. Hasn't been a black and white in this part of town in fifty years, I'd venture.

"Two minutes!" the pilot barks at us, his hands and feet continuing a complicated pas de deux with the collective and the rudder. They are shooting at us now, the chopper dips and darts through sporadic love notes to authority, in various calibers.

There is a huge warehouse in the distance, and I shudder involuntarily. Big damn building, forbidding, the chain-link fence down in several spots. More LAPD gunships on the ground there, as well as the coroner's Jet Ranger. A thin blue line crouched at the perimeter of the machines, shooting carefully at the movement beyond the tattered fence, answering muzzle flashes visible from treetop level.

The skids thump down on the baked macadam and we are out, one two three.

"Which way?" Gun drawn, searching, searching.

Derrick motions, then grabs my arm. We are running for the entrance. Our arrival provokes a rush from the perimeter, and the level of gunfire increases. Didi has me tapped into the police band, listening.

"Officer down! Officer down!" To my right a blur of motions whips past the prone form of a cop shot in the thigh; my reaction is swift and practiced. Turn, drop to one knee, aim, don't jerk the trigger. One sound added to the cacophony of battle, one victim punched in the chest with a hollow point, thrown back, a gaping exit wound all he has to show for his machismo.

"Nice shot." Derrick is too casual about killing. We go inside.

The icehouse is a throwback to a previous century, well before refrigeration technology. There are no services in South Centro anymore, and no power company would send people in to maintain the grid. There are blocks of sweating ice, stacked against walls, everywhere, and it is cold. I can see my breath.

"Your stiff is right over there."

I regret the minidress now. The corpse is a modestly attractive woman, five feet two. She is wearing jewelry, not a lot, but what she has is tasteful and expensive, and her hair is cut just so, not a bit on the wild side. An executive secretary.

Totally out of place.

The coroner's boys are monitoring the thermal probes inserted in the body's anus and mouth. They have been discreet, and I can only see a thin wire leading under Riva's skirt. I call her Riva because I am about to get to know her very well. Too well.

"What's the temperature?"

"Ten degrees Celsius." I don't know this one. His

flack jacket says LA COUNTY CORONER'S OFFICE on the back in Day-Glo letters. Someone should tell him not to announce his profession for the snipers who maybe can't read but can interpret Day-Glo as a foot-high bull's-eye.

"How long ago did she kick?"

"Estimate a little more than an hour ago."

Ugh. Without the cold it would have been too late. The thought makes me take an involuntary step back.

"Is there a problem?"

I say nothing, suddenly repulsed by the whole situation. Something is very wrong.

"Don't blow this one, Jenny," Derrick whispers to me. "Waters is paying big for a solve."

I shake him off angrily. "Deeds?"

In my ear. "Yes, boss."

"Ready?"

"When you are." A moment's hesitation. The tiny silvered jacks in my neck are empty and exposed. The boom mike is suddenly cumbersome, archaic.

I take a deep breath, exhale pure white against the chill.

"Okay. Let's get this over with."

I reach down and touch Riva's cold, cold flesh.

This freak show is the result of my one enduring talent. I am a former piggybacker, current telepath, so powerful that I can take residual thoughts out of dead flesh just by the touch of my hands. So far I have ignored the babble of voices in my head, the intrusive thoughts of others secondary to my locus of concentration on Riva Barnes. There are limits, even to my ability. This cursed talent is a residual of my first meeting with one Derrick Trent, and I resent him for it to this day.

Her skin is alabaster cold, marble. I brush a wisp of her hair away from her forehead, closing my eyes as I do so. I shudder, not from the cold, but from . . .

"Talk to me, Jen." Didi's voice is far away.

. . . entry. The mosaic is grey around the edges, gaps forming as her brain chemistry breaks down past the point of no return. Only her last thoughts are accessible, dimly perceived.

She isn't in the icehouse when it happens. There is *pain*, incredible pain that is pushing my eyes out of their sockets, a glimpse of a paneled room with lots of knick-knacks in glassed cabinets.

The room spins, staring at the ceiling, and she cries out, her pleasant voice turned malevolent by the pressure in her head. What is it? What's doing this to her? Involuntarily I shrink into a crouch, fetal position, staring at the carpet.

There is something there.

The vision fades to purple, fuzzes out. I am back in the icehouse in South Centro, primitive gunfire sporadic at the edge of hearing. The floor is slick with condensation.

"Deeds?"

"Still waiting, boss."

Shit. "Help me up, dammit."

Derrick lends me a hand, pulls me too close. "See the perp?" he asks gently.

I shake my head, no. "She wasn't killed here, though."

Coroner's office: "How can you tell?"

"The place was different, a house, maybe a mansion."

"And?" This coroner's man is a disbeliever.

"And what?"

"That's it?"

"Yes. That's it."

Derrick is looking at me closely. If he sees the lie he says nothing. I wrap my arms around my chest, trying to stay warm, my pistol sucking heat from me into its cold metal.

"Okay," Derrick says uncertainly, "let's wrap this up and get the hell out of here."

"I'll wait outside."

"Not on your life."

"Then put me in a chopper back to my office."

"Cool your jets, Jenny."

"I want out of here. NOW."

Derrick sighs, exasperated. "Fuck. You start charging by the hour?"

"I don't need to." Don't, and I mean DON'T, fuck with a skittish ex-piggybacker.

"Okay. Be a bitch."

I do not look back to see the late Ms. Riva Barnes being zippered into a body bag.

My favorite line of all time from a two-d movie: "Earl here tried to pork me." I forget the movie.

Back at my apartment: I need a stiff drink and a couple of downers. Jesus, what a freaky scene back there. I know that Riva had sex shortly before she was killed, because I could feel a man's sticky wetness between her legs. She was naked when the bastard killed her. I know it was a man. I know it was a lover. Damn shame no one cared about DNA evidence anymore. Not since cops started coming up with artful ways to introduce bodies to genetic markers that supposed perps couldn't possibly have put there.

Derrick Trent, homicide detective, LAPD, tried to pork me many months ago. I find it terribly odd to think of it now, because the reference doesn't quite match.

Trent brought me into the department, helped me clean up the wreckage of my life. From there we'd gotten close working on a couple of cases. They were beginning to call us the goon squad, he on the inside, me on the outside as a paid consultant. One day out of the blue he touched me, and I backed away.

My talent is ubiquitous. Since that night in Heaven ten years ago, I can't turn it on, I can't turn it off. The background babble is bad enough, I've said that. But one touch, even a light kiss, and I am there, inside someone's deepest thoughts. I couldn't make love to a man who could have no secrets from me, and I could see all of Derrick Trent's secrets in the blink of an eye. I could smell all the other women he'd ever been with, all the other fantasies, all the nightmares . . .

No, no, no. Sorry. I have enough of my own. I don't need his or anyone else's, at least not for free.

I tried to explain it to him and I think he understood. But he watches me now, wondering if it was all a line, part of the axis of mutual suspicion between normals and capables, watches me to see if I'm seeing someone else.

But I can't, I can't. My life is barren, my apartment is barren. There are no secrets from Jenny, but Jenny has one. All this body and looks, all delectable but no one to sleep with. Normals sicken me, and I look at Derrick now—

—and turn away.

Later after the booze and pills and the tears, I can look at myself in the mirror and begin cleaning up the damage. It's always like this after a job, the wretched feeling that is never compensated by the fat paychecks. I wonder if I'd piggybacked with that loser back at the icehouse if I would have seen myself in his thoughts; I wonder what the reflection would be postmortem. An arrogant, cold blond bitch with a gun, the muzzle flash from a decidedly phallic pistol the last thing he'll ever see, not even his last dying thoughts held in private on the way to hell.

I wonder if it was that way for Riva Barnes's killer. He's like me, you see, even more powerful.

I can tell.

The reports will read no visible cause of death. Massive spontaneous trauma, instrument or instruments unknown. He killed her and dragged her into South Central, into the icehouse, so that they'd call me, so that I would find Riva Barnes and look into her mind. A frightening thought. My fame has spawned a killer. A resourceful killer, a powerful madman.

Unbidden the vision floods over me like a storm, the pain, the grey scales of her fading memories, the paneled room with the glass cabinets, falling, falling, falling into the plush carpet, the pressure intense, crushing, rolling to one side to ease the pain, staring at the carpet. And seeing the nape of the pile shift, wobble, and break into a pattern, letters forming out of the orderly fibers, a name:

JENNY 6-ALPHA 23799

My name. The killer has sent me a Valentine's Day card purchased with a normal's corpse.

There have been two others.

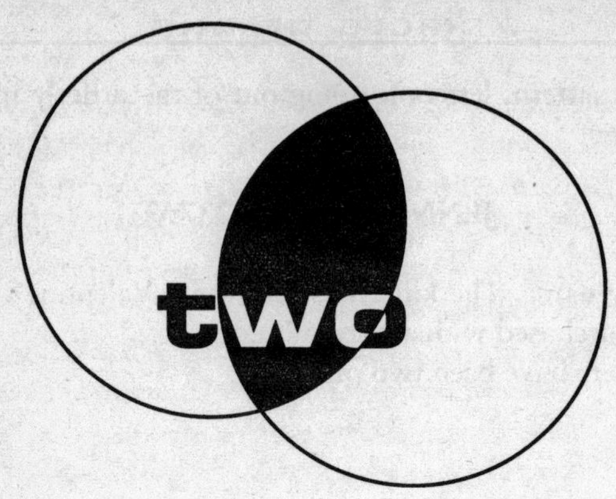

the boy has to be a man. he has to stop being a child sometime. when is he going to grow up? when?

he needs to apply himself. stop being a bitch.

stop being a bastard. don't hit me again, you shit, i'll divorce you.

look at him. the pillsbury doughboy. he eats chocolate syrup right from the can.

He wandered away from home for long periods, it was easy. He had some friends, they had money. He didn't have a girlfriend, though. Girls thought he was weird.

and that fucking dog! christ! have the help take it out and kill the goddammed thing, would you please? sissy. strong men. strong men, that's what i need.

suck my . . . shut up you little bitch, i can get it better at the office.

shit that was good. suck chrome from a bumper, girl. better get out of here before the battle-axe comes home, shut the door. oh, only you. what're you looking at?

Stim was a mind-blowing experience. Punch in a fantasy, pop a pill. Surround sound reality, sex with goddesses, change the program when you got bored.

Maybe fiddle with the chip a little, heh, heh, maybe override some of the safeguards, up the voltage just a teensy bit, maybe do some stuff that was (hey!) contraindicated alongside, surf the wave on top of the wave, hang ten, dangle your thing. He knew how to get the money. Who needed women?

he likes niggers, you know. had a baby bat in his pants over that black bitch in his class. jungle pussy, ass out to here, titties like fucking hindenburgs. he's your son, he must have picked that up from you—like i don't know what goes on.

like i don't know what goes on! goddammit! again and again, that's what goes on!

wrinkles don't do it. make your mark, think you deserve a little better in life, everyone has a taste on the side, they fuck like bunnies at the office, hire 'em because they get down on all fours during the interview . . .

He took Riva with her skirt on, just like she liked it, put his cock in her so she squealed a little when he pushed past her lips, did something with her mind, made her think, made her feel more than he was capable of feeling about her. Stripped her clothes off when she wanted him to. Thought about the nigger girl in high school, now she had a nice ass.

Thought about Jenny. Thought her name.

Jenny 6 Alpha 23799

Drained himself in Riva, letting the demons out of

his head to squeeze Riva past the point of consciousness, oh god, oh god,

Oh Jenny.

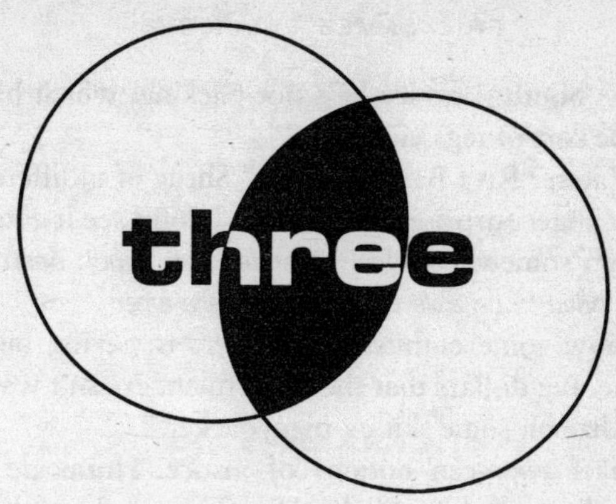

Sylvia's. It's a place in downtown, it's the day after Riva turned up cold in Mr. Right's homemade morgue with a thermal probe up her privates. I'm waiting for Derrick, not a small inconvenience. I hope that this meeting he called me for is brief, because I don't feel like Nancy Drew today; this morning's headache is a doozy. The bad ones come more frequently these days.

Derrick comes in, wearing a monosuit that looks as if ultrasound was never invented. Unbidden, my mind reaches out for him over the constant babble of background noise so common in a hash house. Oddly, I get nothing in return.

"Long run. Wish they'd open up the freeway again."

"Last quake like'd to take out half the Pacific Coast highway, man. You don't wanna be runnin' a load of soy up that sumbitch anyway *<money, lots of money in that>* if it's gonna give." The truck drivers are behind me, somewhere.

"Jenny." *Nothing.*

"Derrick." Demure smile. Maybe I'm too tranked up to notice his lust. But he's smiling. Why is he smiling?

"You ready to meet the big guy?" Derrick slithers

into the booth. I notice he's not packing, which has to be some sort of regs violation.

"Waters? Riva Barnes's boss." Shrug of indifference.

His anger surprises me because I don't see it coming.

From somewhere else: *<wonder how much cash is in the till. have to be able to get outta here after . . .>*

"Show some enthusiasm. Waters is paying big for this one. Big dollars that the department doesn't want to jeopardize on some skit ex-piggybacker."

Forget twen-cen notions of justice. Homicide is a commodity just like Micky D's. Thousands of bodies served up every day. You want justice? You pay. You pay big if you want results. Waters is rich. Waters can pay.

"You think somebody else can get results on this one?" I briefly debate telling him my little secret. But no, then I'd have to tell him about the others. All High Profile cases. All failures. Derrick isn't in the mood to hear about my shortcomings. Even I will admit it's time for a solve. Certainly my bank account could use a lift. What money I have is getting lonely for fresh new playmates.

"LAPD is thinking about bringing in another consultant." Derrick smiles a big smile just for me. What's with him?

"Yeah?"

Bigger grin. "Yeah. And you didn't know that, did you?"

If he knew it, I should've known it. Why?

He sees indecision. Triumph licks the corners of his lips.

"It's Masque, Jenny. Waters and his people will be using it when we go in."

Masque. So that explains it.

The grin turns wicked. He practically pulls a waitress into his lap to get ahold of her coffeepot.

"Gotta go easy on the stimulants when you're on this stuff, Jen. Great shit, though. Department's making it SOP on piggybacker cases."

"Why Waters and his people? They want me to solve this thing, or what?"

Derrick carefully places his black coffee back in its saucer. "Waters is a big-time wheeler-dealer. Industrial secrets. Business deals. Who knows? Maybe there's something in his head that you could use against him."

"Like his whereabouts when Riva got snuffed."

Derrick shrugged. "Cash he's paying, the captain regards it as an instant alibi." He reached into his pocket and slid a wafer-thin chip across to me. It sits in the no-man's-land between us, the glint of processed silicon barely dulled by the micro-thin plastic coating.

"I take it these aren't your mash notes to Stim junkies."

"Nope. Waters Industries. Everything we have on the place. Most, but not all, gleaned from public sources." He looks at me expectantly while he sips.

Let sleeping chips lie, I think, the purity of the instinct too compelling not to run with.

"Well? Aren't you going to jack it in?"

"No. Rather meet the man first. Get some initial impressions and ratify them later with the cold hard facts. I don't know much about Waters right now."

"You should do your homework, Jenny. You solve this one and we can both retire."

The way he's looking at me raises the hairs on the back of my neck. There's a dangerous, unspoken converse to his statement. LAPD wants the credits. No holds, no rules, no loyalties. Just produce a killer and a payday. And Derrick Trent, if the scuttlebutt is half-true, hungers for paydays.

And if a certain consultant has the willies, well, redundancy is the name of the game.

Worse, this Masque shit has just raised the stakes.

Waters Industries is out in the valley, a smooth black obelisk of opaque glass and shock-buffered steel. The cab glides to a stop on titanium rails, the building is way beyond the radius restrictions on p-transport. We are far away from the mayhem of the inner city, of South Centro, far away from where Riva Barnes was deposited like a satchel of unwanted goods. There are sprinklers for the lush, chemically treated lawn and the fines for that kind of irresponsible irrigation must run to thousands per week.

Derrick is calm as we are checked through security. He isn't packing because the guard looks like he would think nothing of kicking a cop's ass if that's what the order of battle required. With everybody wired from the inside, metal detectors are passé without serious pattern recognition software to distinguish the resonance of deadly intent. I hope they don't scan for listening devices; Didi couriered me a stick pin with full motion video and sound recording capability so that I can record the meeting for posterity. I'm plugged in, too, the sockets at the base of my neck leading to slender gold-impregnated cables that slink into my jacket, and from there wireless into Didi. No finicky boom mikes today.

The building is a low-rise, maybe ten floors. We are escorted by a guard to the top floor, by my (lousy) reckoning we are in the southwest corner of the building.

The carpet is slate-grey and sumptuous, straight out of executype decor 101. A vast oaken workstation stands empty, swept clean of papers and memorabilia, Riva's station, an impossible maze of slides and controls and displays and other shit that looks like it came from the bridge of a bad *Star Trek* knockoff.

The only babble I get is from the temp, who is too busy eyeing the blinking boards with utter confusion. There is but one office behind the oak tree, and the door is closed.

I focus, and I get nothing from beyond that door.

Nothing.

<record start.>

<taping now, boss.>

"We have an appointment to see Mr. Waters."

Derrick has the badge in his hand but the beleaguered Kelly girl waves it, and us, away. She strides briskly to the closed door, knocks, and opens it a crack. She doesn't know how to buzz inside, and I can imagine the poor wretch wearing a patch in the carpet going back and forth. Derrick is calm, the only tension visible to me is the hunch of his shoulders and his worried glance at me. Fucking piggybacker, don't blow this.

Poor Derrick. Masque or no, he is deluding himself if he thinks anything beyond that door can provide the keys to the promised land. Cops are cheap. Capables are cheap. Men in shiny suits hiding in executive suites are cheap. If you don't believe me, ask one how long it would take for some other shiny suit to be sitting in their chair and fucking their secretary if things don't go right.

The door. It swings open on gimbals, like a section of the wall opening up on a secret compartment. Arnold

Waters is a large man, florid and white-haired. He is older, maybe in his sixties, and his surgeons have done a nice job on him. The paunch suggest jowls that aren't there. The complexion suggests baggy pouches under sunset-red eyes that aren't there either.

"Detective Trent." The voice is mellifluous, neither threatening nor standoffish. There are two others in the room, Waters's people. Derrick submits to a stupid little half bow as if he's meeting the dead queen of England for the first time.

"And this would be . . ." the voice ends in a question, the eyes are on me, cool and dark blue.

"Jenny Sixa." I use the shortened version of the alphanumeric designation that all capables suffer through. Unlike Derrick, I offer my hand, which Waters doesn't shake. Instead, he takes my hand warmly as if he were grasping a debutante whose pedicure merited a kiss on the knuckles, a subtle bid for ownership if the price isn't too high.

The pin is wide angle vid-capable, although the picture degrades at the edges of the arc. I turn to the younger of the two Waters men, the standees, to let Didi digitize better.

"And you would be?" He is handsome, younger, in his thirties, and expressionless.

"Richard Waters." He at least shakes my hand limply. If he had glasses he'd be Clark Kent handsome.

"My son and number two man." In the company, Waters adds tonelessly.

"And you?"

The other is owlish, polished down to the acrylic on his fingernails.

"Jeremy Bentsen. Outside legal counsel for the company."

Patriarch, line of succession, blocking back. They are all Masqued, untouchable.

"Shall we get down to it?" Bentsen's retainer obviously doesn't quibble about billable quarter hours.

There are chairs around a coffee table next to the office-length picture window. There are brown hills in the distance in the petrochemical haze; there are dozens of little p-cars in the parking lot.

We settle. "Tell me about Riva Barnes," I ask quietly. I can tell that Derrick is irritated by the shift in his shoulders. Everything I wanted to know about the victim is on the still unscanned wafer in my purse.

Waters begins. "She's been with the company for eight years, straight out of college. Been my executive assistant for the last four. Quite a loss, too, from that point of view."

Efficiency is a prized commodity here. "Where was she from originally? Dose she have any family?"

There is a moment of silence. Waters clearly doesn't know. Interestingly, it is Richard who clears his throat and answers:

"Back east. A small town in Pennsylvania. Parents are still living . . . She has a brother, I think."

"A brother . . . here? Or back east?" Focused on Richard now. No hint of guile.

"Back east."

"And she worked for you, also?"

"Me? Oh, no. Dad's very possessive of his staff."

"And her social life?"

There is another silence, longer this time, and shifting in chairs.

"I realize that this information is already digitized and scannable. Context, however, is not. If my questions seem redundant it's only because you may have information in your heads that may provide a lead."

"She was an attractive woman. I believe that she had an active social life." This from Bentsen, precisely the wrong source for that kind of information.

Derrick: "Is there someone on staff that she was close to? Who can provide details about who she was dating, for example? Who her friends were?"

Arnold looks at Richard, who answers. "Possibly. We can certainly check. Do you think she was killed by someone she knew?"

Derrick: "Something like this is usually a crime of passion. A personal motive can't be ruled out."

"Hmm. I see." Arnold is looking out the window as he responds.

"And can you tell me about the nature of her work for you, Mr. Waters? Did she have access to sensitive records? Business dealings? Anything that might lead someone to kill her?"

"I'm not sure how to answer that, Ms. Sixa. Surely, Riva had access to a great deal of sensitive information, information that could be quite useful to our competitors."

"But you were happy with her work?"

"Absolutely."

"And you trusted her with sensitive information?"

"Of course."

"We do have," Richard says, "an internal security force and rather tight controls on the dissemination of sensitive data. A large part of our confidence is based upon how zealously our security people do their jobs."

Are they zealous enough to kill?

I pause for a moment, letting it all sink in.

"I apologize for not having done my homework on Waters Industries. Could one of you give us a fast overview of the company's business?"

"Richard?" Arnold is now clearly bored, a unique position for a man being asked to discuss his empire.

"Well"—Richard takes a deep "where do I begin" breath—"Waters Industries is an international conglomerate. We have interests in mining—"

<17 percent of last year's gross, boss.>

"—electronics—"

<22 percent, boss.>

"—and other heavy manufacturing concerns—"

<equity interests—unconsolidated.>

"—as well as a number of partnerships in various research and development efforts."

"Government contracts?"

"Some, again, primarily in R & D."

<military subcontracts were 15 percent of the business, boss.>

Richard pauses, looking at his father. Arnold says nothing.

"What's in this building?"

"Administration and corporate offices, mostly." Arnold is looking at me, gauging my reactions.

"Anything else?"

Arnold shrugs. "There might be a business or two that we've left out. Nothing major, though."

<wrong, boss. That list is only 54 percent of last year's gross . . .>

<shut up, deeds.>

"That all seems rather . . . boring, doesn't it?"

Arnold smiles. "Business, Ms. Sixa, is never boring."

"I have one other question."

The four of them look expectantly. "Why are you using Masque?"

"Jenny, I thought I made it clear . . ." Derrick is indignant, but Waters waves it off.

"Ms. Sixa, I realize that you're on this case because of your unique talents. However valued and trusted Ms. Barnes was to us, she was still just an employee. None of us"—careless wave at the others—"are suspects, therefore your unique talents have no use in this room, in this setting. On the other hand, each of us has in his head information that you have no business having, not to mention intimate personal thoughts that most people would be embarrassed to reveal."

"So," Bentsen, now, "you can see that Masque is only a logical protection for us, and for you. It's a brutal world, Ms. Sixa. Information can often be lethal in the wrong hands."

Score one for the not-so-subtle threat. Masque is a drug that alters the neurotransmitters the brain boys say are the key to my telepathic abilities. It makes them unreadable for a duration of one to five hours, depending upon the dosage and the physiology of the user. That means Derrick is getting close to the edge of his envelope. No telling where the others are on the curve.

"Do you want me to solve this case?"

"Ms. Sixa. Of course we want justice. Do you want to stay healthy?"

Arnold, Arnold. Brazen is just not your style. I look at him and every ounce of my body language says "Fuck you."

"See? You have, as I just did, asked an intuitively obvious question. I suggest you turn your talents toward finding the real perpetrator of this crime. We, like Riva, are simply tertiary victims of an act of mindless violence."

<who manufactures Masque?>

<waters industries, boss.>

Keeping it all in the family, as it were.

I guess we're done. I stand, and the men stand, a certain sense of relief in the room.

"Before you go, Ms. Sixa, there is some paperwork, I'm afraid."

"Excuse me?"

"We're requiring a confidentiality lockout on disseminating information concerning Waters Industries or Riva's life and untimely death."

"How extensive?"

"Life times five," Bentsen says smoothly.

"That seems a bit extreme."

"It's a requirement for all our consultants. Just a formality, really."

<deeds?>

"I work on the explicit condition that my findings are only made available to LAPD."

<working, boss.>

"Not good enough, I'm afraid."

"Mr. Bentsen, I've worked on dozens of cases that were much more sensitive than this one. I'm sure you've checked my history. Nobody but the police are interested in my findings."

"Makes no difference. I've advised Arnold that there

is no way a capable should be turned loose on this without some safeguards."

<they use a lockout to keep you from getting into their records, too, boss.>

<shit.>

Richard tilts his head. "Ms. Sixa? You are aware that we cannot continue without this?"

<deeds, pull everything you can from the public nets RIGHT NOW. bend the rules, anything . . .>

"Can I have a moment to think about this?"

<more like ten, boss.>

"No." This from Bentsen.

Richard is whispering into his sleeve. "Security, Mr. Waters's office right away."

"Okay, if that's the way you want to play it."

"Security is on the way up here, Dad."

<how long, deeds?>

<working, boss.>

"You will get some people on the staff to talk to me about Riva, won't you, Rich?" I give him a killer "I want to tear your clothes off" smile.

"Of course." An iceberg.

Security hustles in with a black box.

<deeds??>

"Who?" He's a killer, this one. Bulge under his armpit, balls of his feet stance. He either gets my prints or he kicks my ass in a nano.

"Her." Richard points to me.

"But not Derrick?"

"Already interdicted."

Security crooks a finger at me. "C'mere."

Yessir.

The black box opens to reveal a flat panel sensor

screen. Space for both hands. They will interdict me by my prints first. Security activates the equipment, and I feel a slight buzzing that translates up my wrists.

<just lost three quarters of the nets, boss . . .>

Retinal scan next. Security clamps goggles over my eyes. "You know the drill. Won't hurt a bit."

A reddish light moving right to left.

<dumping off-line.>

<make sure you pull the chips.>

<already done, boss. on-line copies are being wiped by the interdiction. resets are in.>

Security removes the goggles, dumps the feedback into the base. He studies readouts flashing in the air.

"Well?" Richard.

"She's obviously wired for sound and video. We cut her access fifty-three seconds into a massive search of the nets probably initiated from here."

Derrick acts theatrically appalled. Security smiles.

"We got all the data, though. All of it."

Arnold Waters breathes a sigh of relief.

"Oh, and Missy?" This to me.

"Yes?"

"We cut you off when you walked into Mr. Waters's office. You haven't been talking to your office at all. You've been talking to one of our Artificial Intelligence programs. The transcripts should make for interesting reading."

<deeds?>

"You mean . . ."

"I mean that fifty-three seconds of access time was a theoretical number. You actually got nothing. Not a damn thing."

Jee-sus. These boys are serious.

Security packs up his tools. "Oh, and by the way."

He would grin while he dismembered a toddler.

"Say hello to 'Deeds' for me," he says as we are escorted out.

The least of my worries is Derrick's genuine anger. Didi confirms my worst fears—the link fritzed out right as we walked into Arnold's office, and no, she cannot get anything about Waters Industries from any source on the planet.

Even my internal processor has been interdicted. A gigabyte's worth of information and imagery from the meeting is buried somewhere in my head and completely inaccessible. I am left with only my organic memories of the meeting and any notes I can commit to a piece of paper.

And Derrick's dose of Masque is wearing off. The ranting and raving are coming through on all levels now, an annoying buzz that complements him screaming at me.

"Are you trying to blow the goddammed case? Waters is probably on the phone, right now, talking to every fucking politician in the county to get my ass fried for having brought you in in the first place!"

I shrug. Let him vent.

"I mean, going into Waters Industries wired for sound and vid? Trying to beat an interdict? Have you lost your mind?"

"You're acting like I was supposed to know that these people had their own damn high-tech Gestapo."

"Waters Industries, Jenny. This is the big leagues.

The Big Leagues. Couldn't you tell from the setup? They had their lawyer in the meeting, for God's sake!"

And how did they do it? They must have been onto me as soon as we walked through the door. They must have fed my few words with Didi into some really big machine in the basement, shaked it, baked it, and slapped their own feed over my encrypted net, and made it sound like Didi and I were on-line without missing a beat. That takes a cryoprocessor with a lot of power.

In fact, it takes power that nobody is supposed to have.

"Are you sure that Arnold isn't into computers?"

Derrick shakes his head. "Not even close."

Hmm. Truly interesting. They bought something that nobody else has, just for their security systems? Sometimes the prefix "mega-" is an understatement.

"I'm telling you, Jenny, if Waters doesn't like somebody, he can make 'em disappear."

"Then how come he isn't a suspect?"

Derrick looks grim. "I've thought about it myself."

"And?"

"And if he is, then he's paying several million credits for us to find somebody else to pin this on."

"It would appear."

Except. Except. Waters isn't a capable. None of the people in the meeting were telepaths. And none of them had the slightest hard-on for me. A serial killer? One of them? Mass murderers I could see, if not imagine that it's already happened. But a serial killer? It's the one thing that confirms Arnold's innocence. It's the one thing that only I know, that Derrick doesn't know.

Then what the hell are they hiding?

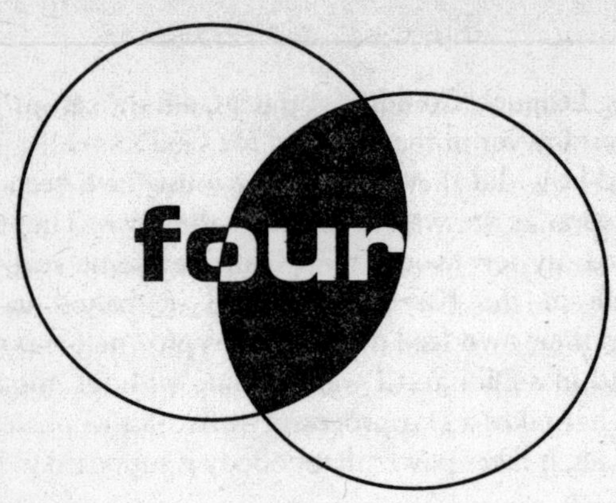

The weight of our numbers depresses us, the need for hierarchy within the social matrix condemns us evermore as the scale between our numbers and our resources tips in Satan's favor. We cannot be as individuals, we cannot be as part of the ruly mob. Our very need for order condemns us to chaos.

—Unknown Twen-Cen Philosopher

Returning to LA proper was depressing, even without the load of bad news from the day's events. There was a stage 3 pollution alert, which meant that you were required to wear a mask. Mine quickly clogged with gummy, wet black soot, like some ozone blasted inversion layer of burnt rain forest. The crowds, the wretched crowds, were clingy as they always are when the air turns that foul. One would have thought that we could condemn our problems into areas without law like South Centro, but just the opposite is true. The open sores infect us everywhere, on the streets, in the air, in the very nature of things—if one cannot build a big enough cell, then society as a whole must serve that function.

Secretly I welcomed the babble from their immune

blasted systems; I welcomed the discordant keening of their humanity more than the cold, cool hush of footfalls on thick carpet. They were more openly human and festering than all of the executive suites in the universe where mankind bleeds more quietly into someone's repository of wealth. Karposi, Tuberculosis Five, Aggressive AutoImmune Breakdown Syndrome. Sickness and disease with a name, a known enemy, myself to join them in some never-never time dimly hoped to be far from now.

Derrick assured me before I left the cab that Riva's Records Autopsy, which consists of the standard download of her phone records, banking, and credit transactions would be ready sometime the next day. Small bits of flesh for a case that suddenly looked as if whole sections of the skeleton would remain missing. Damn.

These cases were never easy. Even a good glimpse of a perp copped off a victim was not enough by itself to track someone down. It was starting with the end point, the result, and working backward to trap a suspect in a web of confirming evidence, a way of winnowing out those leads until the infinite number of suspects could be narrowed to a circle that included only the killer. I wish I could simply bump into someone in the street, read his thoughts, and triumphantly denounce him as the solution to one of the hundreds of unsolved capital crimes in the county each year, but the courts have already thrown out cases schemed by obvious shaman who would point the finger at anyone—for a price.

Instead, using a capable is prejudicial to the wheels of normals' justice, an inherent suspicion of less than fair play. We are not allowed anywhere near a courtroom for fear that one of us might reveal the intimate thoughts of a juror or jurist out of context and make a mockery of the process. But for all the handicaps, it does help narrow down that circle of infinite possibilities.

In my office, my private one, with Didi sitting outside, I go through what Deeds calls symbolic therapy. I diagram cases endlessly, looking for some clue that makes all the information make sense. On heavy construction paper with a crayon, I draw a circle with three names inside—

Riva Barnes
Genevive Wilkerson
Marie Folcoup

Three women, three bodies, all tattooed with my name, listed most recent first. To the list inside the circle, I add two additional names—

Riva Barnes
Genevive Wilkerson
Marie Folcoup
Jenny Sixa
Mr. Right

I've checked. There is no intersection between myself and the others. Outside of the circle, I write the names of the big three at today's meeting—

Richard Waters, Arnold Waters, Jeremy Bentsen

and of course,

Waters Industries

No, no, that doesn't feel quite right. Waters Industries deserves a circle of its own. New paper, new crayon. WI in the center.

No data.

I color in the outside of the WI circle with black crayon, angry, dark, and depressed.

No data.

I wonder if Derrick has any information—

Wait. WAIT. He does have information.

He gave it to me.

He gave it to me on a wafer. And it's in my handbag.

"I *told* you to scan that thing."

"Screw it, I'll scan it now."

"You can't."

"Sure I can, Detective. I'll just pop it in the reader . . ."

"It's time and date stamped. Keyed to your ident. Your ident is interdicted. Dammit, Jen, you should have scanned it when I gave it to you."

"Wait one. *Deeds!*"

Didi walks in. I like my robotoids (she hates it when I call her that—the proper term is Artificially Intelligent Being, or AIB) cute and courteous. "Yes, boss?"

Derrick's wafer sits in the middle of my desk blotter like a cookie. "Derrick gave me this before the interdict. Can we scan it?"

Didi swings her head back and forth. "We can't even scan *topics* related to Waters Industries. I've tried. No go."

Damn. "What if we got someone else to scan it?"

From the phone: "*Jenny . . .*"

"It's keyed to your ident. Even if we found somebody

to break the encryption they probably wouldn't be able to read it."

Deeds. Since when have I ever hesitated to go around the bend on something?

"Get Ada on the phone." Ada is my pal, my buddy, and my favorite net-bender.

Derrick: "Jenny, give it up. It's just a wafer. We have written summaries . . ."

"Yeah? How many pages?"

Hesitation. "Few hundred or so."

"Thanks. That does me a lot of good. You going to quiz me on it when I'm done memorizing a few hundred pages of copspeak?"

"Better than nothing, Jen. And right now, you got a big-assed handful of nuthin'."

Punch the button. Put him on hold. Big-assed handful of nothing. The construction paper is a funeral wreath of black around a circle with Waters Industries in the center.

Didi, blessed Didi from the outer office: "I have Ada Quinn on line two."

"It's time and date stamped. Keyed to your ident . . ."

"We can't even scan topics related to Waters Industries, boss . . ."

"Acquaint her with the problem and courier over the chip."

"Got it, boss."

Ada can bend it. I know she can. But there's something else cooking in the old noggin, something . . .

What is it, a Venn diagram? Set theory. High school logic classes.

Of course. Invert the universe. Invert the search.

* * *

Later that evening . . .

"Anything from Ada, Deeds?"

"Not yet. Give her some time, boss."

Hmm. "And what about your little project?"

"Working, boss."

Best thing about an AI is that they don't complain about long hours and they don't get overtime. Didi has been clicking away at her keyboard on what I call the null search. It works like this:

Take a list of business topics, say widget manufacturing, hydroponic gardening, whatever, and access the nets for information on that topic.

"We can't even scan topics related to Waters Industries, boss . . ."

Anything that's interdicted has to be something related to Waters Industries. So by default, we can at least sketch out some of the things that Arnold and the gang of three are into.

Next, and even more inspired, I had Didi order up a hard copy (yes, I know, how *quaint* . . .) of *Who's Who in American Business*. Say we can't access info about widget manufacturing. Okay, now we look up Mr. Bill Wadbucks who happens to be the head of the Widget Manufacturers association. Let's say the nets come back ***Access Interdicted*** on Mr. Wadbucks.

Bingo. Now we have a name, because Wadbucks is a public figure with no other reason to be interdicted except because of some association with Waters Industries. Get it?

Better Didi than me for keyboarder's cramp. Yes. She has to take notes on all this. On an old typewriter we whistled up from some junk dealer. (Asshole wanted fifty bucks. I told him to get stuffed, but Didi probably got him down to twenty. She's like that.)

So every time I hear the old Selectric going, I know Didi's got something.

Isn't this fun? It's like going to private eye school. Samantha Spade, Private (no) Dick.

And with Ada on the case, maybe we can make some real sense of this, even beyond what's on Derrick's little chit.

It's now eleven o'clock in the evening. Third cup of cappuccino from the machine down the hall. I told Ada to call me when she was about to quit for the night, and knowing Ada as well as I do, I should be getting a phone call any minute now . . .

Line one lights before the instrument chimes. Oh, little lady, you are just too bright for this world.

Didi over the intercom: "Boss, there's an Erasmus Trainor who wants to talk to you. Says it's urgent."

"Erasmus who?"

"Trainor. He knew you were here, even called me 'Deeds.' "

Weird. "Put him through."

"He's on a vidphone. I'll put him on the center wall."

The center wall turns translucent. The man, flinty, is familiar. Very familiar.

"Ms. Sixa."

The security guy from Waters Industries. I don't like this. I don't like this at all.

"Yes, Mr. . . . Trainor? We weren't exactly properly introduced earlier."

When he chuckles, and he chuckles now, I imagine small animals clinging to their mothers deep in the forest.

"Well, this is an opportunity to get to know me better."

"Not exactly something I was anxiously waiting to do . . ." Line two is blinking; the phone chimes.

"I think you should get to know this side of us real well." He has something in his hand, something smooth, black, like a tiny transmitter with a button.

Didi: "Uh, AQ on two, boss."

Ada . . . "Split the screen, Deeds. Tell her I'll be right with her."

Half of Mr. Trainor waffles, then fades until his image re-forms on the right side of the wall. Ada, on hold, waves to me. She is seated at the center of a massive tangle of equipment. Ada is in her fifties, with longish grey hair and glasses, of all things. I always tell her she looks like a granny turned radical feminist . . .

"So what do you want, Erasmus?"

"At approximately 4:45 PM this day you had a data chit containing sensitive information about Waters Industries delivered to 8959 Sepulveda."

"Don't know what you're talking about, Razzy." Jesus. He knows about Ada. What's he getting at?

"Ten minutes ago, we detected a sophisticated bypass of certain net safeguards designed to access the same data chit you had delivered to Sepulveda." He's really got me nervous now. What is that thing he's playing with?

"We were able to backtrack and confirm the extrusion came from that selfsame address. We also confirmed that an Ada Quinn, a known associate of yours, was the source of the extrusion."

Erasmus Trainor leans forward into the pickup. The transmitter key prominent in his right hand. "You see, lady, we don't fuck around. You can kiss your friend good-bye."

He presses the button. A red light on the top of the flat black surface of the device is the only evidence that he's transmitted something. Christ, could it be . . .

I punch the hold button for Ada's line to pick up her call . . .

"Hey, hon! Look, I think I got something . . ."

"Ada, get the hell out of there!"

"Huh?"

"Get the hell . . ."

The vidphone pickup at her end tilts crazily as the blast rips through her room, through her flesh. As the fireball expands the picture collapses to static. Trainor's image is gone, faded to a pinpoint of light, and the dead signal from Ada's funeral pyre greys out the entire wall with electronic snow.

"NO!"

A heartbeat, maybe two, before I believe what just happened. God DAMN these bastards. God DAMN them! I have Didi get LAPD on the horn to tell them to get over to Ada's house, get the trucks rolling, damn, damn, damn, nothing could have survived that.

Damn.

But I have that motherfucker on vid, I have him down to his shit-stained shorts. By God, when LAPD sees the tape of this . . . I personally want to be there to throw the switch.

I pull out my keyboard.

Recall, call sequence, last two, display, split screen . . .

Working . . . the wall says.

Ada's image, on hold, comes up first, left-hand side. I

can't bear to look at her. The right half of the wall transluces . . . displays not Trainor's stinking face, but:

Access Interdicted. Security Code #574930

Waters Industries

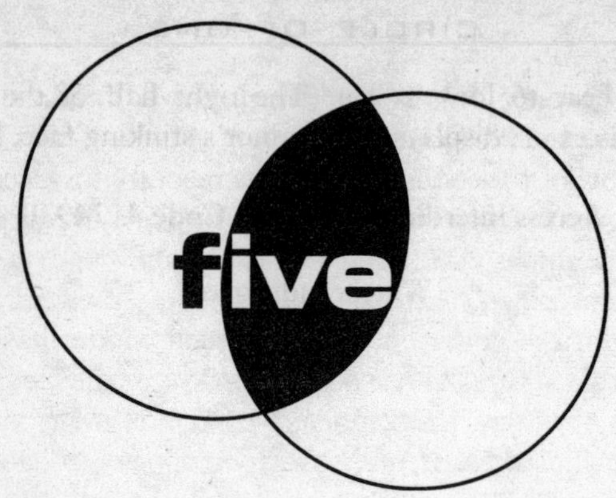

They pulled her out of the utter devastation of a building that would ultimately be condemned. Ada Quinn's charred body passed by Derrick Trent and I on a last journey to the morgue, via the coroner's wagon.

"Plastique," Derrick says in that shorthand he uses with information that I may not give a damn about. "Shaped charge slapped on her front door—it blew inward. She never had a chance."

I nod, numb to the buzz of thoughts around me, numb even to Derrick's unshielded thoughts of concern. *He wants to hug me . . .*

I can't take my thoughts off of the gurney. Ada Quinn, brilliant woman, blown away because I'd tempted fate for her.

She lost. And I'm still here. Even if I'd warned her she would have run to her front door, right into the center of the explosion. She was a dead woman the minute Erasmus Trainor called me with a detonator in his hand, dead probably from the time they followed the courier out of my officeplex to her door.

"Wait." I say this not to Derrick but to the men carrying Ada's remains into the ambulette. I have talents, cursed talents. This is one trip that Ada Quinn should not have to take alone.

"I want to see the body." The men are disgraced by what seems a fantastically ghoulish desire. Derrick, behind me thinks *<shit!>* and shrugs at them.

The roasted flesh smell is intense as they unzipper the plastic holding coffin. Movement in the bag suggests that several of her body parts were collected from where they lay dismembered in the remains of her apartment. There is one square centimeter of clothing clinging to what was once her torso—I touch her right under there, settling into the pattern of her brain chemistry, what little remains, willing myself to connect with the corpse of a friend.

I can feel what she felt, the fear at my warning, the sudden rush of adrenaline, and then the horrible ending after the explosion, life roasting away in the fire.

Derrick has to pull me back to break the connection, but my reaction doesn't stop. Horror at the intensity of Ada's death pushes at veins in my head, a drumbeat that doesn't stop as Derrick shakes me, shakes me, drums of pounding blood flowing through constricted arteries, like nothing I've experienced before.

Dizziness.

Then darkness.

"Your word against Trainor's. No vid, no nothing. Courts don't give a damn about affronts to capables or their friends, Jenny. You know that."

"I love it when we make excuses for the way things are."

"Are you going to be okay?"

"What are you gonna do about it if I'm not? Kiss it and make the hurt go away, mommy?"

"Whoa, Jen. I'm trying to be helpful here. I'm on your side, remember?"

"Yeah, Derrick. Sometimes I am prone to forget that."

"Well, try not to do anything else stupid." We are back at my office. Didi is in the front doing something efficient. I've got my feet propped up and an ice bag on my head. Trent slipped me a mickey of cop-approved happy juice just to make sure I'd feel okay.

"How about this. *Deeds!*"

"Yeahboss."

"Get Waters Industries on the line."

"Dammit, Jenny! Didi, don't put that call through!"

"Uh, Detective Trent, I don't work for you. Switchboard is on line one, Jen."

"Tell them I want to talk to Arnold Waters about the case. Now."

"They say that Mr. Waters is 'in conference' and can't be disturbed."

The old fart works late, eh? It's quarter to three in the morning.

"Tell them it's an emergency."

She whispers into the pickup, a sound so soft and directional that neither Derrick nor I can hear what she's saying. "They're putting the call through, Jen."

My front wall flickers, stabilizes into the image of not Arnold Waters but his progeny, Richard.

"Can I help you, Ms. Sixa?" If he notices my wretched condition he shows no sign.

"Yeah. Your vaunted Security just killed a good

friend of mine. I want to know what the fuck you're going to do about it."

Surprise, genuine surprise. He's still dressed sharp as a tack, although I don't remember if he's wearing the same clothing from our meeting this morning.

"I'm not sure I'm hearing this right, Ms. Sixa. Our Security did what?"

"Erasmus Trainor. The neo-Nazi thug who put the interdict on me? He called me up this evening, said that I'd broken the interdict, and said he was going to kill a friend of mine who was helping me do exactly that. Two seconds later she was killed by a bomb placed on her door."

But Richard is not listening to the last. He's whispering to someone off-camera.

He turns his attention back to me. "And you have a recording of this call?"

"I'm interdicted, remember? No records access. Nothing. Probably wiped clean the moment he signed off."

Richard blinks twice, turns away again.

"Who the fuck are you talking to!" I explode.

The vid pickup on their end pulls back. Arnold Waters is sitting in a casual jumpsuit. I can see now that they are in his office.

"He's talking to me. What time did Trainor make this alleged call?"

"Eleven or so."

"And he implied that your friend was in some danger?"

"He didn't imply a fucking thing. He said, and I quote, 'You can kiss your friend good-bye.' Then he pushed a button. My friend didn't even have time to blink."

There is a pause. The two potentates exchange glances. Something in their looks suggests that this isn't the first time that WI "Security" has gone unsanctioned.

"That is a very serious charge, Ms. Sixa."

"And my friend is seriously *dead*, asshole." Arnold actually flinches a bit.

Smoothly, Richard Waters interrupts. "I know you're upset. However, without proof, the only thing that we can tell you is that we will investigate this on our end. You have my word on that, Ms. Sixa."

For a heartbeat he looks right into my eyes, as phony a suggestion of sincerity as I'll ever see.

"The proof, *Mister* Waters, is in the LA County Morgue in little pieces. Didi, cut this line before I get even sicker."

They fade to black.

"Who was Riva Barnes?" Richard Waters has supplied some names from the company's staff. This one, Julia Logan, is a redhead, short, and way too thoughtful about her answers.

"She was . . . nice. Conscientious."

Julia isn't using Masque. "How long did you know her?"

"Year and a half."

"How did you know her?"

"I work for a section head who reports to Mr. Waters directly on certain things."

"So you knew her from the office."

She nods.

"Socially?"

"We weren't best of friends." *There is a coldness here, not just a lack of caring . . .*

"So you can't tell me about her social life."

"She didn't seem to be . . . promiscuous or anything."

<I wonder if the rumors were true . . .>

"She have a boyfriend?"

<married, or unmarried?>

"I think so. I'm not really sure."

"And her work performance, as far as you could tell?"

"Fine. Mr. Waters is a very demanding person to work for." *<he'd probably run you around the boudoir a few times, honey, but you ain't his type . . .>*

"Did she ever mention being in any kind of personal distress? Financial problems?"

"No."

"Obscene phone calls?"

"No."

"Family problems?"

<all she talked about was her hick roots . . .>

"No. She was close to her family."

"She have any hobbies or special interests?"

<is she supposed to be some hotshot crime buster? . . . stupid blonde> "She read a lot . . . she went to church, too." *<heh, heh. maybe I should tell blondie here she was a virgin!>*

Enough.

"So what is Waters's type?"

"Huh?" *That got a rise out of her.*

"Was she sleeping with Waters?"

Flustered: "I never said that!"

"You didn't have to. Honey, didn't they tell you who I am?"

"A consultant working with LAPD."

"A capable. You do know what that means, don't you, Julia?"

"You mean . . ."

"Is she supposed to be some hotshot crime buster? . . . stupid blonde . . ."

"Oh, I . . ."

"Shall we try this again? Or would you like me to tell you something more personal?"

There is an image in her mind. A man, perhaps her boss, telling her to be careful what she says to me.

"Look, I really don't have much more to say."

"You haven't said very much up till now. Fine. Go back to your desk and practice being a good little peon."

Oh, that was smart, Jen. Really smart. Start a cat fight with the first one you see. Guarantee that no one says anything to you.

The day wears on. I see ten Julia Logan types who have varying degrees of nothing to say about Riva Barnes. Not even any dirt, except for the recurring unspoken theme that she was shtupping Arnold.

It makes me wonder if Erasmus Trainor had her killed because she was a lousy lay.

Donald and Patricia Barnes are gentle folk who live in a time warp called Chicoppie, Pennsylvania. They are both understandably upset about Riva's death. Most of the initial twenty-minute conversation is spent keeping both of them from tipping over the emotional edge. Neither of them is coming to Sodom to claim her body.

With the parents my tactics are a bit different. I couldn't ask her coworkers any of the sensitive questions because I knew in my bones that those interviews would be reviewed in 3-dimensional detail.

"Did Riva know any telepaths?"

Mrs. Barnes: "Not that we know of. She wasn't that kind of person."

"What kind of person?"

"The kind that runs around with those . . . people." The circus freaks, you mean? Like me?

"Did she keep in touch while she was working here on the West Coast?"

"Oh, yes. Donny, we must have talked once or twice a month, wouldn't you say?"

"Yes. Maybe more. She always used to come home for Christmas."

"I see. And has the level of contact decreased at all in the last, oh, year or so? That you noticed?"

Blank looks. "I don't think so. She was very busy at that job of hers, though."

"Did she talk about her job much?"

"She couldn't. That's what she told us. She found it all . . . exciting, I think."

"She say specifically what she found exciting?"

"Going to different functions with her boss. Traveling. The money she was making."

"She say anything else about her boss? Have you ever met Mr. Waters?"

"Not much. He did send us a note, when she was . . . when they found . . ."

"Do either of these names mean anything to you: Genevive Wilkerson?"

They shake their heads.

"Marie Folcoup?"

Nothing. No tie to the other victims. I have to admit that I'm not good at serial killers.

I'm reaching here, searching for something, anything. "Do you have the note that Mr. Waters sent you?"

"Yeah. I'll get it." Mrs. Barnes and I simply stare at each other while Mr. Barnes is off-camera. "Are you okay, Ms. Sixa? You don't look well."

"I'm fine," I say too quickly. Mr. Barnes returns, thankfully.

He reads the note. "I feel terribly responsible for your loss. My condolences. Signed, Richard Waters."

Hmm. Interesting. Richard isn't her boss. They might not know the difference, though. And Richard seems to be the type who does the little things that the patriarch doesn't have time for.

In some ways they are remarkably resilient, these oakies. Mrs. Barnes is on the verge of losing it several times during the conversation, Mr. Barnes has no tears that can express his sense of loss, or his guilt at not having protected his daughter. They both seem lost, as lost as their daughter is to them, all the wonder of life turned into a deadly mystery, their view of the universe and their part in it turned upside down.

And I wonder—is it justice that we seek? The Barnes don't mention punishment. They don't seek vengeance. I wonder at the calculus of their indigo mood, the volume of their space darkened by a killer's shadow. I envy them their darkness, just as I despise the unwanted intimacies of a thousand strangers, their footsteps pounding in my head, pounding . . .

And if not justice, understanding? Comprehension? Some almighty lesson to be learned, a terrible truth from a willful God?

I wonder.

That night I think about the Barnes, about being the kind of person that Riva Barnes didn't associate with. The circus freaks. The capables. *I wasn't always a telepath. I wasn't always a freak.*

One summer when I was fifteen we spent time on the Incorporated Jersey Shore with the fat touristas and kids of all ages. If ever there was a group desperate to have fun we were it.

We walked the beaches early in the mornings, the wind erosion pulling grains of sand across the endless expanse like tan smoke. The beach was wide, the surf crashed muted against the Plexiglas pollution barriers two hundred yards out to sea.

"The beach is so long I'm gonna walk and walk and walk and look up and see myself coming from the other direction!" Shouted against the wind it was a reasonably stupid thing to say. The beach was so clean, I thought, careful to step over the dark oily smudges on the sand. So clean, and so big.

The Incorporated Jersey Shore was the biggest thing I'd ever seen that wasn't fucked up with concrete. When the wind shifted you could even hear the flames billow from where the black greasy smoke palled directly up from the sea, a sound somehow more crisp than the hollow crash of the surf, more like ripping rippling silk. If you looked hard you could even see the actinic slash of the flames within the black carbon mass of offshore smoke, like a welder's torch left on and fueled from some bottomless well of gas emanating directly from the ocean's waves.

My dad lit a cigarette as the black cloud washed over us. It was eerie in the cloud, with the sound of the surf sucking sand and no light, just for a moment. When the light returned it was like coming back from an adventure.

Dad looked down at the beach. "Here." Mom and I spread the blankets and ran to get beach chairs from the vendors who hawked them. Set them up as Dad lit another smoke.

"Gonna walk," I said and he nodded. He closed his eyes and went to sleep without making me wear something over my bikini, just as good because I wanted the boys to notice me. Gonna walk. Gonna walk until I meet myself coming back the other way. I liked the feeling of sand under my feet, shiftless, endless sand. I liked the smell of the ocean, the salt touched with decay and gasoline, maybe touched as well with the scent of light sweet crude from the pyre offshore. The drill cranes in the distance from the petrochemical recycling complex reminded me of home and the rusted oil well pumps that moved up and down, sifting through the sand.

There were other people, of course. Old men like my father, nursing narco habits and gaggles of children gawking at the black mass emanating offshore, a carney atmosphere inherent in being this close to the elements. The Atlantic was primal, voracious, eating away at the beachfront and at man, entertaining in its efforts. The blown well had been burning for four years and too much time, money, and lives had been spent trying to cap it without success. Maybe a nuclear bomb would do the trick, was the current thinking.

The black cop's uniform was the same khaki color as the beach. He smiled at me as I asked him where I could get something to eat on the boardwalk. I tried not to look at my distorted image in his mirrored sunglasses.

"Sure, kid. Most everyone goes to Surfside. Half mile down the boardwalk. Five minutes if you catch the tram car."

"Thanks, officer."

"Your parents know where you are, right, kid?"

"I'm fifteen, officer . . ."

"White. Bob White. Kind of a joke. What's your name, kid?"

"Jenny."

"Okay, Jenny. I know you won't be my missing person report for this hour, right? Because you're fifteen and responsible."

"That's right."

"Okay. Surfside's the place." He was gone for an instant as the black cloud swooped in from offshore and I wondered whether I would see only the whites of Bob White's eyes.

I did not.

It wasn't Surfside that fascinated me. It was the fun house, one of many on the boardwalk. It was the boy flying a kite on the beach nearby. He had long hair, he was beautiful.

"Yo, watch the strings." I was cutting across the beach to get to the fun house, which sat on an outcropping from the main boardwalk, a fingerlike extension that pointed toward the ocean.

"I said, watch the strings!" I finally looked down because he was talking to me. He was reefing in line from his kite, getting ready to launch it again into the stiff onshore breeze.

"Sorry," I said, trying to be as coolly apologetic as I could in that "poor, clumsy, beautiful me" way that screamed that I wanted him to notice me.

"No problem," he said, and flicked his wrist. The rig strapped to his forearm snapped and whirled and the kite leaped into the air. It was fluid, it was sexy. He watched the kite and me behind his sunglasses.

"Nice rig."

"Ever flown one before?"

"Nope. Looks easy enough, though."

He pulled down his shades to get me a high attitude look, *avec les grande octane*. "Yo. Style is never easy."

Well excuse me.

"Wha's your name?" he said, reaching his other hand across his body to shake hands with me.

"Jenny. Yours?"

He grinned. "Kyle." He bowed just as he did something with the rig, and the kite dipped precisely as long as he did. "At your service." He straightened up and the kite soared, a rippling Dacron parody of his movements.

He had long chestnut hair that caught the wind and a muscular, wiry body. I thought of all of him as a kite, ready to catch the wind.

"Here, hold my hand."

"Why?"

"You can get the feel of the kite by holding my hand. Don't worry, it won't bite you."

I grasped his hand, the one with the kite rig on the forearm. We laced our fingers together as the kite darted in the sky laced with black wisps from offshore, the tension in his arm from the string not the only stirrings I felt coming from him. And that in itself was weird.

I felt him getting turned on by me.

I *felt* him.

Later when Kyle had his rig put away we sucked down some yogurt shakes at a franchise. Officer Bob saw us and waved.

"Hey, Jenny. Not missing yet, right?"

"Nope. Officer Bob, meet Kyle . . ."

"We've met," Bob said, and his voice was quiet.

Kyle did his now stupid-seeming half bow anyway. "Off'cer."

"Take care of yourself, Jenny. Remember what I said. Fifteen and responsible, right?"

"Yeah, sure."

Bob laid a curt nod on my date. We were off to the fun house.

"Yo, so you don't hold your breath when the witch cloud comes?"

"Naw. I'm from LA. It's always like this out there."

"Damn. Never been to fuckin' LA. Always wanted to go."

"You surf?"

"Little bit."

The boardwalk at night. Lit by sodium vapor lamps that gave it an orange tint, vendors hawking everything. Cheap prizes for games of skill and chance. Franchises, water rides, T-shirts, first aid stations for people not used to the sulfur content of the black witch cloud blowing in.

And kids. Kids hanging, drifting, smoking cigs and goofing on the touristas, playing their friends for kicks, trading insults. Some of the girls looked at me and Kyle like we were the perfect couple, and I felt lucky.

"So this is the fun house?" Sometimes you ask an obvious question to get the conversation to a higher plane, sorta to give the guy a straight line to work from.

"Yeah. You got some credits, Jenny?"

"Sure." Of course I'd depleted myself buying hair boy here a yogurt shake thick with franchise markup. I plunked three dollar coins in his hand.

He nodded. "Then let's have some fun."

The bad thing started in the hall of mirrors with Kyle holding me close. We stepped in and there we were, reflected in a million different directions, our images refracted into tiny slivers of ourselves.

"S'cool, ain't it?"

It was making me dizzy. Kyle and me, him standing behind me with his arms wrapped around my bod, his hands hooked into the belt loops on my jeans. You could turn your head a little and see a different angle, turn again and see another side, look up and see the reflection from the back . . .

"Give a lisson . . ." He put headphones on my ears, hard guitars in my head, and he was on me, tongue down my throat, smelling of hot fudge and opiated nicotine, his hands running up my torso to my breasts still encased in my suit top under my T.

In that instant I took that walk down the beach and met myself coming the other way—

<wanna do her. wanna do her bad.>

but it wasn't me talking. No fucking way.

Don't know how I got back to the hotel the next morning; woke up wearing the same clothes with the same sand rubbing the same places raw. Woke up sprawled on the floor of my room, the door barely closed and pushing against my flip-flops with every touch of the wind outside.

The maids wanted in, and I felt like I was surfacing from a deep well. I shoo'd the maids, took a quick shower, smiled appropriately when Mommy and Daddy opened the door connecting the two rooms. Yes I had a good time. Yes I'm hungry. Here, Daddy, an ashtray.

The bad thing came back to me fuzzy and indistinct as we hit the boardwalk in search of breakfast. Everything on the Incorporated Jersey Shore is a greasy spoon during the summer. Might as well eat breakfast within sight of the panorama it cost so much to come see, right?

Except for the bad thing. There's a commotion on the boardwalk ahead, hackles on my neck raised up at the flashing lights of an ambulance and police electrics pulled to the edge of the boardwalk, men huddled in a group on the sand below the wooden planks. Dad pops another cig and I'm thinking of asking him for one at the sudden headache I have, fuck the lying protocol about teenage smoking. I need a fucking hit, and I need one bad.

Black Officer Bob White is standing on the boardwalk waving people around the police and emergency vehicles. Something's on the beach, covered up, flash from a photog's light gun washes out the flare from the burning well offshore. The flash continues to blind and hurt me, slowing down time and motion and thought. Bob White's angry voice telling us to keep moving, his eyes on me and me alone until he looks back to the bundle on the beach. I catch a hint of something—can't go there—from the blanket.

"Get your family the hell out of here, mister!" Officer White says angrily to my father.

"What's the commotion?" Dad asks, looking for some way to ditch a butt.

"Just keep moving, okay, pal?" Officer Bob looks directly at me, pins me with his look in a way I don't like, almost as if I can hear what he's thinking, which I especially don't like because of the way his voice and his body language seem to form a question that I cannot bear to have asked, much less answered.

And right there in front of Mom and Dad, Bob White hugged me while I cried.

There is a stack of papers on my desk the next morning, clean crisp IBM selentric type. Ah, this is Didi's notes from her search. Very good. Passes the weight test. Perhaps I'll start by reading LAPD's summaries about Waters Industries and Riva Barnes.

You know what a pain in the ass it is to read? Forget the phony cyberpunk stuff. I want to scan, cross-tab, collate. Even dumb computers are good at that sort of thing.

Take Riva's personals. I have a printout of every phone call she made in the last six months. It isn't a long summary. If I get Didi to match off Riva's phone bills to people on her interdict list, maybe I'll have something. Give the little AI something to do, y'know?

There are some interesting things here, though (if you call a few cups of coffee and eye strain interesting, that is). One of the business segments missing from the LAPD report but included in Didi's interdict list is something called Biomechanical Manufacturing. Didi tells me it's not the same as cloning, apparently. We could dig up a hundred terabytes on *that*.

Let's look at Didi's "people" list. Under BM there's only one—Phillip VanMeer, CEO of Celludyne. Low points for originality on the company name, Phil. Didi has his phone number listed next to his name courtesy of a printed reverse telephone directory. Hmm. Two phone numbers.

Let's just punch up the first one. Stand back, Deeds, I can handle this . . .

"Celludyne Manufacturing?" This is one of the obnoxious Artificial (doofus) Intelligence mail systems that gives you four hundred options before you're allowed to press "O"perator. Clearly that one is the office. Presumably the other one is home, playpen, personal, whatever.

Let's take a peek at Riva's phone bills. Toward the end, last two months.

Not surprising. A single match on the biz line. Meeting's canceled, calling from home, no big deal.

Now isn't this interesting. One, no, at least two matches on the other number. And that's from a random scan. Doesn't necessarily mean anything—I mean the other number could be his helicopter or something. Remember the old maxim—if it has four legs and runs fast, think horse, not zebra.

As a matter of routine I look quickly for Genevive's or Marie's home phone numbers. No matches that I can tell, but this is another thing that Didi can tell me.

I read through the LAPD summaries some more. Waters Industries is well connected, newsfax photos of Arnold with luminaries, politicians, the governor of the state, and the vice president, a voluminous, indexed appendix of legal cases brought by and against the company . . .

And Riva's personnel file from WI.

Okay, standard summaries, age (twenty-nine), height, weight, salary (really good for being a young gofer, I see), and job history showing what I guess is a decent amount of upward secretarial mobility. Short comments from Arnold about her performance, nothing sexual from either him or the rest of the file.

Model employee, churchgoing (if I can believe that bit of info), close to Mum and Dad.

Obviously, sex is missing. And obviously, Riva Barnes had sex before her death.

Let's see the autopsy. Cause of death . . . etc., etc. "Victim does not appear to have any contusions or abrasions consistent with violent assault." Fingernails were clean, no tissue samples there, nails whole and unbroken. No physical indications that she resisted the sexual advances of whoever last slept with her.

If she was killed by a capable there wouldn't

necessarily be any evidence of sexual assault, at least externally. In fact, being done by a capable is at least consistent with unprotected sex. Consistent, but not conclusive.

She either has a steady boyfriend with whom she is comfortable au naturel and she lives on the wild side of immune deficiency risk, or she was forced by Mr. Right telepathically. If she has a boyfriend, why hasn't he come forward? Why doesn't anyone know about him?

I convince Derrick that we should take another look at the icehouse. He bitches and grumbles, but eventually agrees to get us choppered back into the Dead Zone. Not a Daussault this time, but a regular LAPD black and white. Not even a gunship.

Derrick is cool for this trip. I sense that he's hiding behind his pharmaceutical security blanket, that maybe some of the heat that he was expecting about me has come down on him. Whatever it is, he's all business.

"You guys come up with a boyfriend?"

"For who?"

"Riva."

"No."

"You don't find that odd?"

"Maybe she was in-between lovers."

"Great. You got any ex's I can talk to?"

"No."

"Lighten up, Trent. I feel like I'm playing Double Jeopardy or something. Have you found any evidence of a love life?"

He shakes his head. "That important?"

"Good-looking woman. Her profile is decidedly weighted to the 'purity and light' scale of things."

"So?"

"What if she wasn't what she appeared?"

"What? Like a Stim fiend with a thing for violence? The beauty of the system, Jenny, is that you can do anything you want in your head."

I have this wicked flash of Derrick hooked up to a juicy megabyte marked SEX.

"No boyfriends, then."

"No boyfriends, no lesbian liaisons."

The chopper banks low on approach. The zone is calm today, and I can see the icehouse through the perspispex canopy. The fence is repaired. There are workmen moving huge blocks of ice into battered delivery trucks.

There is a ring of sentries armed with weapons.

We set down in the parking lot in the middle of sullen faces. It wouldn't take much, maybe a slight change of circumstances, for the guns to be trained on us. A man in blue overalls and a heavy coat (it's in the high seventies today) sprints to the chopper. He does not look happy.

"You did call ahead, didn't you?" I ask Derrick as the blades slow. He waves me off, and I take that as a yes. We step down out of the chopper.

The name patch under the coat identifies the man in blue as Zack. One of his boys chest passes a shotgun to him. "You did call ahead, didn't you, Derrick?" I whisper as Zack pumps the shotgun. Of course he called ahead. Zack looks like a busy man who doesn't like interruptions.

"What the fuck you want?" Zack asks.

Then again, maybe he didn't.

Zack is a bushy black man with tinges of grey in his mustache. It is cold in the icehouse. Zack props his feet up on his desk in the office and snicks his chair back a little to be closer to the electric heater.

This hasn't started very well. In an age where "institutional" racism has become "inherent" racism, I get all the markers from Zack's head about white cops invading his turf because some white bitch turned up dead in his place.

Derrick is all "official business," thinking that some mighty whitey head trip is going to move this man to be cooperative.

"This is a working establishment." Zack doesn't want us wandering the floor. "We got rules."

"This is police business," *nigger*.

"You're a long way from downtown." *<didn't give a fuck that eddie got shot that day . . .>*

"Uh, Zack, hon." He looks at me like I'm less than poor white trash. White police trash is more like it.

"We just want to take a look around. We might have missed something when the body was discovered."

<like eddie . . .> "My customers don't like blood on the product."

I take a risk. "Maybe I could give you something . . . for Eddie's folks?" I have cash, a fifty, tucked between my thumb and palm. Zack sees it before I place my hand flat on his desk.

Zack holds out his hand. I shake it.

"Deal."

And he palms my fifty with Derrick never the wiser.

The white chalk outline is faded under the tire tracks from the forklifts moving Zack's product. We begin with the outline at the center and move outward in a spiral. I'm staring at the floor. Derrick and Zack are next to me.

"How did Eddie die?" I ask Zack quietly.

"That day the woman was found. Eddie was the night guard. We found him out back after you people left." After the shooting finally stopped.

The floor is slick and cold, with a thin coat of slush in some spots. I don't remember it being this cold when Riva was found.

"The generators went down when the shooting started. Place probably warmed up pretty quickly."

We are walking in a circle about twenty feet in diameter from where the body was found.

"Was Eddie a friend of yours?"

Zack shakes his head. "Eddie was a sweet old man. People left the place alone because they didn't want to hurt Eddie."

There is a wall of ice that I don't remember from before. We are thirty feet from the chalk outline.

"So how was he killed?"

"Shot down like a dog. One in the chest, one in the head." He looks sideways at Derrick. There is a little history here. Two, maybe three years ago there were a series of assassinations by two LAPD detectives in South Centro. Whether it was drugs or graft, I don't remember. The signature wounds were a bullet to the chest and a bullet to the head, both wounds invariably fatal. "To serve and protect," the dicks called it. Each would fire one of the shots to make sure they were in each killing together. People took to calling them S & P hits. Even now, multiple gunshot fatals are called S & P shootings.

"This ice wasn't here two days ago, was it?" I ask. Zack shrugs.

"You don't move it out, it melts," he says simply.

"So what did the police report say about Eddie? Any leads?" Zack shoots me a "bitch, are you crazy?" look. No wonder he's pissed. For effect, I shake my head in bewilderment.

"That's the way it works."

I think it is important to stand for a moment in silent tribute to the "sweet old man" who probably stood between my killer and the ideal place to put Riva Barnes's body. I need to set Zack up for some work. I'll follow up on Eddie's killing later.

"Can we get these blocks moved now? Just for a sec?"

Zack looks dubious. "Whoever killed her probably killed your Eddie. You know that, Zack."

"What I know is that LAPD protects its own."

Derrick has the good sense to keep his mouth shut. "I'm not LAPD."

Zack processes this. Whether he believes me or not, I don't know. But he pulls one of the forklifts from the loading dock to move the ice.

There is another wall of ice beyond, and a gap between two blocks in the lower part of two of the columns. On a whim, I brush the frost away from one of the blocks.

"Hey, Derrick! C'mere." Derrick stoops, careful not to kneel on the cold floor.

"What do you think that is?"

There, halfway imbedded in the edge of one of the blocks, is a black oblong object.

"Looks like, I dunno. A woman's purse?"

Straightening up. "How much do you want to bet that's Riva's purse?"

I'd zoned in on the purse by perusing the personal effects list taken from the body and Riva's apartment. There wasn't a single bag or purse or carrying case that contained Riva's personal effects, you know, all the things that a girl absolutely has to have on hand. I found it extremely interesting that the police had identified Riva by a retinal done on the scene.

It was a long shot that paid off. The killer could have left the purse wherever he killed her and disposed of it at his leisure. But no, he carried her in there with all her effects, probably wedged the purse between two blocks of ice. During the commotion of our first visit, the generators went out. The rising temperature and the pressure from the blocks above partially melted the purse into the block of ice; the condensation re-formed into semisolid ice once the temperature dropped. Derrick has the forensics people going over it now.

Didi has another development. Frederick Barnes, Riva's brother, has finally been located. He's some sort of lumberjack in the Pacific Northwest with a penchant for vacations in the wilderness. He's being flown in; I'll hopefully get to see him tomorrow.

Didi has been working away. All my summaries and

comparisons are in a file that winks at me from the desktop. What I really want is an analysis of Riva's purse and its contents, something is telling me that there may be a clue there.

I also want to set up an interview with Phillip VanMeer. It's an interesting name in an interesting field. It's something that the public nets and LAPD knew nothing about. I'm waiting for VanMeer to call me back, thinking about the way to play it, wondering if he'll be surprised that I know there's a connection to Waters.

The desk chimes once. The telltale indicates that LAPD has sent me a squirt about Riva's purse. Good. Recall the file.

No prints. That's the first disappointment. The killer obviously wiped it down before he hid it because Riva's prints aren't there, either. The rest of it is standard girl and person junk, makeup, driver's license, etc. etc.

It looks relatively complete. I compare this to the personal effects taken from Riva's apartment. No overlap, no redundancies . . .

Curiously, there is something missing. Everyone carries an entitlements card these days. It is better than identification because it carries authorizations for medical care, bank and net access, donor options, the whole nine. It isn't impossible to get along without one, because everyone who exists is doubly recorded by their prints or their retinals. But it is a pain when you need some cash and somebody is holding up the line getting scanned.

So where is Riva's entitlements card? It has no use to a killer, particularly. As soon as Riva was scanned at the scene, her idents and access to all she had, ceased to exist.

"Pull Wilkerson, Folcoup homicide files—personal effects, please."

The deskcomp begins working. It places the two lists side by side on my wall.

"Highlight 'entitlements card,' please."

Searching is superimposed over the lists.

I tap my feet waiting. It seems to take forever.

Items not found.

Could it be that the killer takes a souvenir? The thought gives me pause, makes me leave the desk and stare out the window at the yellow haze.

Trophy? Souvenir? The answer, my answer, anyway, makes my skin crawl. The messages to me in the corpses' thoughts. The placement of Riva Barnes in an icehouse. Entitlements cards. This isn't about "stop me before I kill again." No.

How else will the killer prove his identity to me when the mystery is unraveled?

He wants me to find him.

Phillip VanMeer is an aristocratic type with a bearing far removed from the lab types that make his company go, it seems. He calls me back and Phillip VanMeer materializes on the far wall.

"Ms. Sixa, was it? I was surprised by your call."

"You are in business with Waters Industries, aren't you, Mr. VanMeer?"

"No. We don't have any connection with Arnold Waters or his company."

He's nervous. Even on the vid pickup it's clear that

he's lying because he keeps dabbing at his face with a hankie. He won't even look me in the eye.

"Just let me be sure then. You don't have any business relationships with Waters Industries?"

"No."

"You've never met Arnold Waters?"

"Uh, no. Not that I recall, anyway."

"And, finally, does the name Riva Barnes mean anything to you?"

The flinch, as I call it, is the jackpot. Mr. VanMeer flinches big time at the mention of Riva's name.

"Never heard of her."

"I see. Well, you have my number in case you manage to think of something concerning Waters Industries or the late Ms. Riva Barnes. Otherwise, I'm sorry to have wasted your time."

He nods, but doesn't say anything. He is all too glad to cut the connection.

And he doesn't react to the "late Riva Barnes" tag. Innocent people tend to ask why they are being called about a corpse.

By scrutinizing the homicide stats for the last three years I've managed to isolate seven additional homicides that fit the following pattern—unknown trauma as cause of death of attractive youngish women, ages twenty-two to twenty-nine, entitlements cards not included in the personal effects of the victims. There are others that may be hits as well, where the listing of personal effects found on the victim is too incomplete because of the circumstances.

It was six months between victim one and victim

two. Four months, average, between victims three, four, and five. Three months between victims six and seven.

Between victim seven and Marie Folcoup, two months. Between Folcoup and Wilkerson, two months. Between Wilkerson and Barnes, three weeks.

Three weeks. Mr. Right has a hot hand.

He wants me. Signaling with dead women with little clues in their heads, show-off stuff, hide-and-seek homicide. Marie Folcoup found in her stylish little house in the valley, a vidphone call placed to police 911 with the camera on her naked body. Genevive Wilkerson overpowered in the elevator of a high-rise, the car stopped, and the monitoring equipment showing her body slumped in a corner. The killer climbed out through the escape hatch in the ceiling. Both engendering instant responses from the police and from me. Derrick Trent pulling himself through the hatch in the elevator's roof, showing me how it was done.

"Jen?" Didi over the inter-.

"Yeah."

"Derrick Trent on one. Says it's important."

"Derrick?"

Derrick appears on the wall. "Sorry to do this to you, Jenny. There's a helicopter on the way to your building, ETA five minutes."

Uh-oh. "What's the scoop?"

"Another high-profile victim. This time in Beverly Hills."

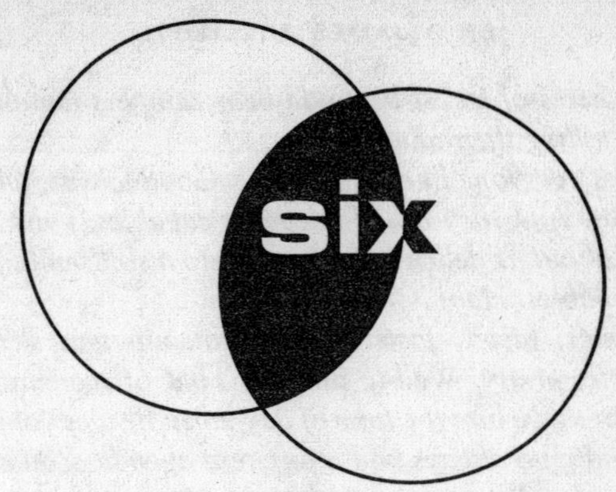

Faster, faster, faster. It's simple, isn't it? Squeeze the components, shorten the instruction set. Cut your competitors' throats.

Same thing applies to life. Your career is a war. It's you against the hordes. You may be comfortable now, but you look at South Central. Look at Harlem in New York. The next ten generations will support those people, right? Get ahead, stay ahead. Fuck the competition. Rules are the tools by which you oppress the people who want your spot. Suckers play by the rules. You find an advantage, you push it, you get some leverage. You see somebody with a good thing, you think, how can I use that to my advantage?

You ever seen a poor high-ranking cop? You have? Then you know somebody that's not just stupid, he's honest.

And for God's sake, if you have an advantage, don't let people know . . .

He started hearing thoughts when he was thirteen. Maybe it saved him from sinking deeper, maybe not. The loudest din was from his parents, that was raw sewage that he'd rather not hear about. But that was everywhere. Everywhere. In the middle of one hundred virgin acres of forest he could hear campers fantasizing about killing their wives.

Was everyone like his parents? Good Christ, what a thought. And they called telepaths capables, huh? Well this is about as delicious as biting into a shit sandwich.

Capables. Hah!

Faster, faster, faster. *Marie Folcoup was slender, brunette, pretty. Well-to-do. The kind of woman who wouldn't give him the time of day when he was younger, the kind who always had a different agenda. You could love her until she made you hate her. You could fawn all over her and she would demand more attention even as she was getting bored. He knew the type.*

She liked friction in her sex. Faster, faster, faster. He'd made her like him, used his advantage to force her into liking him, wanting him. He planted in her mind an impression of his absolute integrity and propriety and found it amusing when she screamed "Fuck me! Oh, shit yes!" during intercourse.

Well he had a different agenda, too. Forced her to keep up public airs, to keep their "affair" strictly private. Closed his mind around hers like a fist one day at her secluded house in the valley and squeezed it to nothing in an instant. Left her naked and spread-legged while he turned the vidphone pickup on her, set the autodialer to dial 911, and, then oh, maybe her parents' house and a few dozen of her friends and business associates. Put her answering tape on the outgoing audio of the calls, "Hello, this is Marie, and I'm not home right now . . ."

That's right, you won't be home anymore. ***Ever.***

Go to hell, bitch.

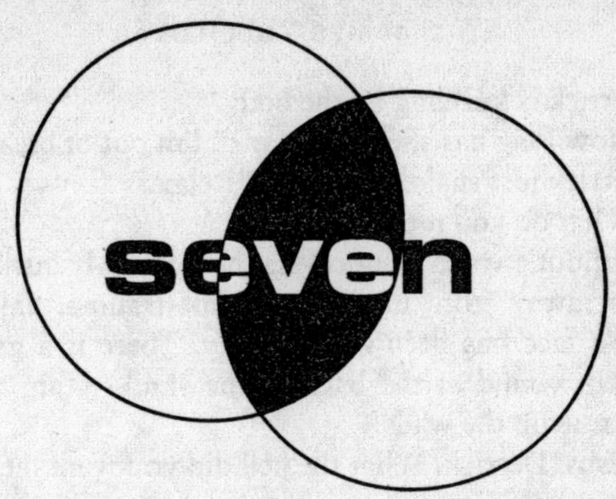

There is a landing pad behind the stylish mansion, a convenient gash cut through the palm trees and denuded, well-kept grass. A swimming pool that looks like they could hold Olympic Trials in it, a full crew of groundskeepers assaulting weeds on the north forty.

Derrick called from the scene; doesn't want to give out any details on an open line. Just me and the pilot who says nothing and thinks about even less. The sweep over the estate indicates that it's really two plots of land purchased and combined; the stream of police vehicles clashes with the stylish p-cars scattered on the streets and driveways below.

A uniformed officer takes my arm and hustles me out from under the prop wash. He is all business too, nervous in a way, thinking about his holstered gun. And we're in Beverly Hills, one of the innermost sanctums of the power elite.

Through French doors to a hidden patio covered with a Spanish tile roof. The first incongruence is the amount of blood that discolors the sheet thrown over the body. Look closely, Jen, because there is evidence of exit wounds speckling the walls.

Derrick is kneeling by the body.

"How long has she been dead?" I'm out of breath.

Derrick just shakes his head. "Relax."

"What do you mean?"

Without a word he uncovers the body. My instinct is to turn away from massive gunshot trauma; half the corpse's face has been blown away. There is a gaping wet exit wound at the back of the skull—yeah, that's grey tissue on the walls.

"Jesus, Derrick. What the hell did you want me here for?"

"Two reasons." He peels the rest of the sheet. "See what I mean?"

Two wounds, both invariably fatal. One in the head, one in the chest. I'm beginning to think that the victim is a woman, although with all the damage, it's hard to tell.

An S &P hit. Like Eddie, in the zone.

"The second reason?"

"The identity of the victim. I'd like to introduce you to the remains of Susan Bentsen, wife of Jeremy Bentsen, head outside counsel for Waters Industries."

Nothing I can do with massive brain trauma; nothing left to connect with. Whatever's left of her brain chemistry is spattered and cold on the walls. I'm staring at her as Derrick tells me some of the salient details—no spent brass at the scene, even though this was a point-blank shooting. Points to powder burns on the victim's expensive sequined smock. Elaborate security systems that hadn't been triggered, house full of servants that severely limit the window of opportunity.

"Is there a guard at the front gate?"

"Nope. Armed response though. Cars cruise the area. They guarantee response within two minutes."

A fucking Houdini-style cowboy did this.

"Clearly she was shot right here."

"Uh-huh. Killer walked up to her, maybe calls out to her softly, then boom boom."

"Anybody hear a scream?"

"Interestingly, no. But everybody heard the shots."

I hear voices from within the house. I recognize both men as they stride from the living room out onto the patio.

"What the hell is she doing here?"

Derrick Trent stands, his hand on his belt, next to his holster. He's on his turf now.

"Ms. Sixa is a paid consultant. She's here on my authority."

"I don't give a fuck," Erasmus Trainor says. "Get her out of here."

Derrick looks to Trainor's companion. Jeremy Bentsen is drawn, visibly shaken. Did he love his wife so much that he's displaying grief? Somehow I don't think so.

<trainor.>

"It's your house, Mr. Bentsen. Do you want Ms. Sixa to help us solve this?"

<christ, all i need is a capable right now.>

"Mr. Bentsen?"

<out, have to get out. get her out of here.>

He shakes his head. "Please . . . please leave."

"Is there something you want to say, Mr. Bentsen?"

<careful! don't think. leave. just leave . . .>

"No. No. Please, please leave immediately."

"You're hiding something."

<fucking pills, get some fucking pills . . . you want into my head, bitch? think about fucking her . . . probably a lousy fucking lay . . .>

"I want to be alone, now." He's staring at me, fear and hatred in his voice.

Without another word he turns and walks away. Trainor follows close behind.

"We need a court order to go after Eddie's body." Derrick is walking me to a black and white. They'll take me back to my office.

"I thought about that. We don't know Eddie's last name."

"Then call Zack."

"I had somebody do that. Hc clammed up. Wouldn't even admit he knew an Eddie."

"Derrick, it's possible there's crucial evidence in that killing."

"And we missed it. Yeah I know."

"So what are you going to do about it?"

"What do you want me to do? He clammed up! He thinks this is some sort of cover-up."

"Call him yourself."

"Uh-uh. I got a better idea. You call him."

"Derrick . . ."

"Look, I can't get involved in a South Centro shooting. Not when socialites are getting burned down in their own homes."

"But it's related!"

"Jen, listen to me. You know the rules. You know

how the department works. We can't have it both ways."

"What the hell do you want me to do? I'm not even a cop!"

"Get me a name, Jenny. Get me a name, and I'll get you a court order."

The electronic ghetto is a reality in South Central Los Angeles. Vidphones require coax or fiber-optic cable that's expensive to lay, and nobody makes that kind of investment in the zone. So I have Didi do an audio-only call to the icehouse when I get back to the office.

Zack isn't around. Didi isn't sure he'll even get my message. I tell her to call him back in an hour if she doesn't hear from him.

Just when I'm thinking it's time to rediagram the case, Didi tells me I have a visitor.

"Who?"

"Frederick Barnes. Says he's Riva Barnes's brother."

Hmm. "Okay. Send him in."

My first impression isn't visual. Barnes is so dirty that his stench precedes him by a country mile. Backwoodsman, okay, but hasn't he been in the city long enough to take a shower?

"Mr. Barnes." I'm afraid to shake his hand.

He doesn't offer it.

Where do I sit?

"In the chair there, Mr. Barnes."

"Thanks." He grins at me with yellow teeth. I didn't hear him speaking the first question.

No, unmistakably, I heard it in my *head.*

* * *

I sit, too, quietly and thoughtfully. His appearance, his smell, and his ability all suggest that I may, just may, be sitting with Riva's killer. Walk softly.

Unfortunately I'm not jacked in. No wires from the sockets at the base of my neck. Damn. I'd feel a lot better if Didi was right here inside my head.

"Why did it take so long to locate you, Mr. Barnes?"

"I was away. Up in the mountains."

"How long have you lived in Oregon?"

A shrug. "Long enough."

"How's the hunting this time of year?"

"Pretty good. Not much in season, though. Small stuff to put in a stew pot, not much more."

So he knows about guns . . .

"Tell me about Riva."

"We weren't close."

"Why is that?"

Because I can do this.

I hesitate.

"She didn't like it?"

Freddie laughs. "When we were kids it turned her on. I'd send her messages in school . . . then it was . . . other things."

"What other things?"

"Images" is all that he will volunteer.

"What did your parents say about this?"

"They didn't know. Didn't want to know about nothing. Not about me, anyway."

"But they were close to Riva."

"Not as close as I was back then."

"And after that?"

"Riva was always the goody-goody kind. They liked that."

"And you . . . weren't."

"Oh, I wasn't bad or anything. I just wasn't perfect. Riva tried to be perfect. That's why she started hating it when . . ."

". . . you put pictures in her head."

He nods.

"Where were you when she was killed?"

"I told you. In the woods."

"By yourself."

"Uh-huh. That's why I go away. Gets too noisy around people."

"And you got here, yesterday?"

"Yeah. Talked to the cops. Derrick somebody, I think. But there were others."

"You didn't tell them about your ability, then."

"Why should I? I came to see you because you know, you know what it's like."

I take a deep breath. How many times has a case been solved by a perp just spilling his guts to somebody who pushes all the right buttons?

"You ever been in trouble before?"

"Not really. Once or twice."

"But you've never been classified as a capable."

He shakes his head, no.

"Tell me about your work."

"Don't work much. Logging is all fucked up by the enviro regs. I work when I can. Wherever I can."

"And you resent that?"

"Maybe. Naw, not really, though. Never liked workin'."

"When was the last time you talked to your parents?"

"A year ago. Maybe more."

The one problem with an ultra capable is that he's not broadcasting much. Normals have to concentrate not to reveal what they're thinking. Capables are too conscious of trying to shield themselves from other people's thoughts.

"Did Riva have a boyfriend?"

"Beats me."

"You have a girlfriend?"

"Not lately."

"Ever?"

He grins. "Oh, sure. I had some women in my time."

I grin back. "Yeah? You wanna tell me about some of your conquests?"

Freddie's grin freezes. He looks away, too embarrassed to put it into words.

I had Riva once.

You had sex with your sister?

He nods.

How many times?

Just once. Wasn't really sex. She was almost seventeen. Virgin. Wanted to know what it was like.

Had you been putting stuff in her head?

He nods.

Images of what? The two of you? Together?

Kid stuff. Fantasies. At least at first.

"And then?"

Then, more . . . personalized. A guy she liked. A girl I liked.

"Explicit stuff?"

Yes.

"And she liked it."

Yes.

"And when it came time for her to experiment, she turned to you. You knew what she liked, what she didn't?"

Yes.

What happened afterward?

She was ashamed.

Ashamed because you were brother and sister?

Yes. Ashamed that she liked it. Between us.

"Did you ever talk about it?"

"No."

"Did it ever happen again?"

"No. I was older. I graduated from school and went away."

"To Oregon."

"Not at first. But ultimately, yeah, I went away to Oregon."

"And Riva came to the West Coast."

He shrugs.

"To be near you?"

"I don't know."

"Did you talk a lot?"

"No. Not at all until way later."

"While she was out here."

"Uh-huh."

"And you were in Oregon."

"Washington, actually. Bumming around Seattle."

"Your paths ever cross?"

"No. Not really."

"Which is it? No, or not really?"

He doesn't answer.

Which is it?

Silence.

Which is it?

Silence.

"Did you kill her because she wouldn't sleep with you?"

"No!"

"C'mon. You can do better than that! Weren't you jealous about the other men she was seeing?"

No.

"How did it happen? At her house? In a hotel?" She wouldn't sleep with you, so you made her?"

No . . . Please. Don't.

Then tell me!

I can't.

Tell me. You came here to tell me, didn't you? You forced her, then you killed her.

"No! You don't understand!"

"Then tell me." *Tell me, Freddie. Tell me.*

He puts his head in his hands.

Make me understand, Freddie.

And so he does.

As I listen to his story I can't help but recall what little I know about serial killers. Riva's sexual history, according to Freddie, was stunted. He cannot recall her talking about a lover until she was in her mid-twenties. And then, Riva Barnes only dated older, wealthy men who didn't satisfy her sexually.

You have it wrong. I didn't want her. She wanted me. You got it wrong . . .

But Freddie has no names for these phantom lovers. He insists that Riva wouldn't reveal their identities to him. I wonder if her last lover was a telepath. One that she found especially attractive because he was a telepath. I wonder if my killer is a wealthy telepath.

It makes a certain amount of twisted sense. Although I haven't studied the new homicides that I dug up from the files, it seems my killer is an organized killer, where organized means some level of capacity to rationally plan and execute a murder that is essentially sexual in nature. Riva, nor Genevive, nor Marie were physically harmed in any way—they were presumably mentally tortured while the killer acted out his fantasies, either in a direct sexual act or in his head.

Poor Freddie. He is mixed up and in need of help, but he is anything but an organized killer. His disheveled appearance, his smell, and, at least in his case, his talent, all indicate some level of mental disorder—if he were a murderer he would be a disorganized killer, one who inflicts horrific damage to his victims, one who doesn't plan as well as Mr. Right does.

It's possible, then, that Freddie's only crime was to predispose his sister to Mr. Right.

If Mr. Right was somehow wealthy. Even organized killers are usually too disturbed to achieve that level of success. Curiouser, and curiouser.

Zack the Iceman Calleth. That's what Didi says soon after spending at least a can of aerosol on airing out the office.

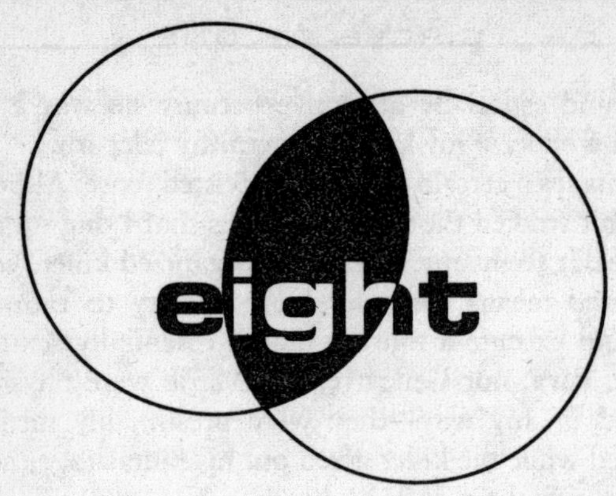

eight

And when you look into the abyss, the abyss looks into you.

—Friedrich Nietzsche

Damage. That's what I think of when Zack Millhouse picks me up at the entrance to the South Centro Zone. Aka no-man's-land, dawn of the dead, and a million others. I don't know what happened to these people, whether we killed them or they put the barrel of whatever gun we offered into their mouths, but this is a barren place, best viewed from on high in HO scale.

Zack has his windows rolled down and the sweet stench of decay fills my nostrils. If LA is disease-ridden, the zone is the blackest of black plagues. There are people sitting on the street side trying to dress open sores that drip copious amounts of fluids and puss; HIV-3 and all the attendant problems are rampant here. A bite from a small boy could be a death sentence—

There are several tykes shrouded in the fog of a small building fire, God's dark-skinned people shrouded in ash. The bubbles of consciousness are fragile, I sense, ready to burst at a pinprick of real or imagined insult.

How many have weapons? Who knows, who knows. Like everyone else they are in their hearts capable of killing, capable of the secret rage, nurtured and preening like a wildebeest, disconnected from the world and from each other, shut out and seething within.

Zack drives, saying little, careful with his thoughts, even.

The scales began to really tip at the end of the twen-cen, when a generation, untold hundreds of thousands, was born into families systematically destroyed by drug dependence and racism. By the time this generation was seven years old they were lost, lost in a nightmare of neglect, of abuse, lost because there was no one around to put limits on their behavior, lost because they were hungry, dirty, and sullen. By the time they were twelve many had already invented a psycho-sexual fantasy world that they lost themselves in for days at a time. By the time they were fifteen, many needed to taste the blood that they dreamed about because the dreams no longer satisfied them. And there was nothing beyond the block but a succession of other blocks with people like them, acres and acres of deliberate strangers who fed off of the same effluent.

By the time they were in their twenties, even the liberals agreed that there was no hope for vast sections of the inner cities around the country, even most middle-class blacks had to turn away from the violence and depravity of an underclass whose only resemblance to them was the color of their skin. The demon nigger of white nightmare became a fully functional reality, dark-skinned deliberate strangers who could kill without second thought, driven not by their humanity but by their fantasies.

And by the time this generation had children of its own the grip of the vortex was so strong that things could only ratchet down, farther and farther. Forever down. Forever down.

Damage. Disease, pestilence, fire, and gunfire. TB 5. Drug resistant and without cure. Karposi wasting syndrome. No cure. Blood that leaked under the barricades of federalized troops into the rest of the world, into the rest of LA and other cities around the country, infesting the underworld and the rest of the world.

And the greatest irony of all? The quiet despair in the nice white society, the madness behind the picket fences, in the executive suites, the emptiness of lives based upon conspicuous consumption or the pursuit of same. The ultimate failure of the American consumerist dream clung to and fictionalized by us all required the legalization of nice white people's prescription dope, Stim, and other mindgames to help take the pain away. *The cage takes many forms . . .*

And of course, my own itinerary down memory lane, culminating in Madam Demarche's bastardized version of Heaven. Entertainment for the rich as perverse as entertainment for the masses, no matter how gilded the circumstances, no matter how frantic the fun. My own damage from that time of soul selling, lingering headaches that never quite leave the edge of my senses, dizziness from my party-girl roots. All that money and all that contrast to this, the dead zone, fucked-up polar opposites that make you think there's no hope for any of us at all.

Zack Millhouse drives with a loaded shotgun across his lap and a satchel of weapons in the backseat. He's taking me to Eddie's last resting place on the hopes that the brave men or women who prepared Eddie for burial can tell me something about the way he died.

After some interminable time Zack announces that we have arrived. Our destination is a funeral home, done in white brick only minimally defaced by the artists in this part of town. The roof is flat, solid. There are long black cars, ancient ones, lined up in front, presumably for a funeral. Like Zack's icehouse, the death biz is a growth biz in the South Centro Zone.

"I'm gonna wait in the car," Zack says quietly. I can only nod as the sound of distant gunfire chatters somewhere. Zack has wisely pulled the battered Chevy around the back of the Carruthers Funeral Home in case the folks who produced the last corpse come around to pay their respects with guns blazing.

There are four parlors where viewings are taking place. To me the rooms are interchangeable, old men smoking opiated cigarettes while the young bucks engage in fiercely whispered verbal horseplay so as not to be disrespectful of the dead. The decedents range in age from fourteen to forty-five or so, more heavily weighted to the younger side of the scale. The sight of me inspires a moment of striking silence as I pass each doorway, a wonderment at the white woman wandering around where her welcome expires every few seconds, like a visa that has to be renewed constantly.

Damage: One of the coffins is shortened to save costs. The body, an adult female, isn't short, but rather was shortened by whatever killed her. I go to the door marked OFFICE and ask for Mr. Carruthers.

The young men sharing some barbecue point me to the desk in the back and tell me to wait. One of them calls out "Pops!" as I sit down. Off to the left a curtain parts and a man wearing a rubberized smock and elbow-length rubber gloves comes in.

"Can I help you?"

"Zack Millhouse sent me. About Eddie? The night-watchman at his icehouse?"

"Pops" Carruthers sits down. "What exactly did you want to know?"

There are a variety of certificates and licenses on the wall behind him, most yellowed with age. The newest, I see, gets renewed every year. It is a license to properly dispose contaminated blood products granted by the Department of Health of the City of Los Angeles.

"What was Eddie's last name?"

"Reynolds. Are you a policewoman?"

"No. I'm a consultant, working for LAPD on what we believe is a related case."

"Lemme see some ID."

I give him what I have, which isn't a whole lot. Most of it is a lame-sounding letter from Derrick on LAPD stationery identifying me as a consultant with the department.

Carruthers hands it back. He is of medium build, with a greying mustache and a thin skullcap of greying stubble.

"How was he killed?"

"Gunshots. Two. One to the head, one to the chest. I think either one could have killed him."

"Did you recover any bullet fragments?"

"Absolutely."

"And where is the body now?" Derrick wants a corpse to do dimensional modeling on the wounds to nail down the type of weapon.

Carruthers laughs. "Eddie Reynolds was cremated yesterday."

Oh, damn, damn. I'm thinking about my next questions when the heavy beat of a helicopter, low and very near, begins to intrude on the space.

"Then I need those shell fragments." The chain of evidence has, of course, been broken. Pops Carruthers could give me the name of the killer, say he found it inscribed on the victim's thigh, and it wouldn't be admissible in court. But if the frags tie in the gun to Susan Bentsen . . .

There is a loud thump from the roof, and what sounds like several booted pairs of feet running just above us.

"What the hell?" Carruthers says, reaching under the desk.

And then the lights go out.

Carruthers is looking for a weapon, hidden somewhere under the desk. In the darkness I can feel his adrenaline as he searches, searches . . .

The front door of the funeral home is smashed inward. My aural sensitivity is heightened by the darkness—I can't tell whether I'm hearing sounds, or thoughts, or both.

<kill everyone.>

<find the woman. make sure . . .>

I can't stay here in the back.

"Is there a back way out?"

"No." His answer is certain in the inky blackness.

I can't stay here. I try to stay close as Carruthers leads the way into the front office. Gunfire splits the eerie silence—a woman screams, drawing more fire. Automatic weapons are going everywhere, and I can hear the slugs taking pieces of the sheetrock.

"Get down!" Carruthers whispers as he opens the office door to the corridor. I mash something sticky and warm with my hand, thinking it's blood, but it's only the remains of the meal the young men were sharing minutes ago.

Someone at the far end of the corridor opens up, a tongue of flame spits from a muzzle as he sprays one of the viewing rooms. Others are killing anything that moves in the other rooms, the floors will soon be slick with new blood. The muzzle flash illuminates one of the attackers—he appears dressed in black, with shoe polish on his face—his thoughts are coldly professional.

Carruthers is a gamer. He shotguns one of the men, blowing him backward, then rolls away as the spit of weapons chews the section of the floor we just occupied. More men are pouring through the crushed outside door, more guns, more targets.

I am silent. Crouched behind Pops I can't get off a decent shot. We are hopelessly outnumbered, and I feel death very near as Carruthers stops and feeds more shells into his shotgun.

Two of the men he killed are getting up, struggling to their feet after taking a chest full of pellets. That means body armor. That means big trouble.

"Pops! Get down."

This requires more expert marksmanship. My gun is free, fifteen shots in the magazine, two spares in my purse. I focus on the locus of human emotions somewhere in front of me—head shots—I'm headhunting now, looking to burn down the odds a little.

There—hollow point to the head, combat roll, rush to the next doorway. Another, stooping down to finish someone in the dark, this one is holding a pistol—two shots because of the shitty angle, back and down, *get down*, bullets fly over my head. Pops takes another in the center chest, I finish him with a roar that obliterates his throat.

<over there!>

Turn and roll, snap three off blindly at the hidden threat, plaster and sheetrock stings with near misses, a threat still active . . . my ankle caught up under my leg, awkward, squeeze the trigger, move dammit! away from the flash and the bull's-eye.

Three advancing toward me. Pops's shotgun erupts once, twice, he's down to reload as the guns speak, one hit one miss, two still up and a foot of muzzle flash visible, and Carruthers has no damn chance.

<that must be her.>

Shoot. Turn. Shoot, turn . . . the third one, the one Pops knocked down is out of reach for a kill shot, the angle is impossibly bad. Go for the groin, twice, and a scream of pain rewards me for my selection of targets . . .

Two more come through. One of them, I think, is the leader, he's methodically disposing of the wounded, I get nothing from him, nothing . . .

Missed one, Jesus that was close, the smoke and the smell of cordite filling the halls now, Pops somewhere behind me, silent, perhaps dead already, just me now, and I count five separate trains of thought that are still rational, still dangerous, and the leader.

That makes six to one. Lousy odds. There has to be a way out the back, a window or something. Crawling back through the halls, yes, Pops is dead alright, so are the two helpers who never finished lunch.

I manage to close the outer office door as the six behind me start spraying the hallway, two high, three low, the leader waiting for a target.

<put the goggles on.>

I stand, hearing the thoughts just behind the door. They are bunched near it, waiting to crash it in and come for me, probably with infrared on now, because I'm the only target left. At the door to the rear I turn.

They kick open the outer door.

Empty the clip. Into the door, into the figures beyond. I'm firing wildly, panic setting in, a waste of ammo. Back into Pops's office, eject the damn clip, search for the replacement, c'mon, c'mon, large calibers shred the flimsy wood behind me, still six of them, still coming, coming . . .

A click, then a soft tinkle as the grenade lands somewhere in the office and rolls against the furniture. Back through the beaded curtain, stumbling over something, the soft *carummph!* of a concussion grenade sends pressure through the opening toward me.

Crawling now, back away from the curtain. A stainless-steel gurney that's heavy, probably laden with a body, around it, get up! Get up! Find a fucking window . . . a bucket of some kind, filled with solvents. I hope. Splash the contents over the floor, light it . . .

Whoosh! A nice smoky wall of fire. So much for the infrareds . . .

At the curtain. One of them sprays the room, the illumination from the flare of his weapon eerie, look for a window . . .

Three of them are in the room now. Their guns cover

the entire space. I can hit one, maybe two, but the others would have me.

There is scant cover here, four in now. Five.

My hand creeps up the wall. There is a pane of glass. A hint of daylight directly opposite me, another window, thick curtains covering it. Six in, gang's all here . . .

"She's in here. Stay cool, let her make the first move. She can't get out."

There is a footstool about a yard from the other window. I can only hope that the floor between here and there is clear.

"Wait a sec—I got her!"

Dammit. Shadows from the flames. Two shots, run, bitch, run, run, run . . .

I stumble on something, damn good thing, because the arc of fire sweeps over me, would have taken my head right off my shoulders. Get up! Get up!

One of them is almost on top of me, turn, pull the fucking trigger, blow him backward, a slight puff from his teeth exploding and gunfire that racks my shoulder . . .

Full tilt to the footstool. Strong leap. Through the window into the light, trailing blood.

The impact with the ground is stunning and unwelcome. My gun hand is empty, my breathing shallow and unresponsive. Shock setting in at the sight of my blood on the brown grass, they'll be at the window any second, and then it'll be all over.

<you're dead now, bitch. heh, heh, heh.>

I turn and see the head for a second, the muzzle of

the gun through the shards of glass. Who are these people? Why are they trying so hard to kill me?

I can feel the thought sending pressure to the trigger finger, an odd juxtaposition, I'm in his head, looking at me on the ground, a sitting target, a bonus to—

—their leader.

The vision ends as the man's head explodes like it was hit with a thunderbolt from God, and Zack is there, strong arms under my shoulders, dragging me away to his car. He smells of gunpowder from the discharge of his shotgun, and I am glad.

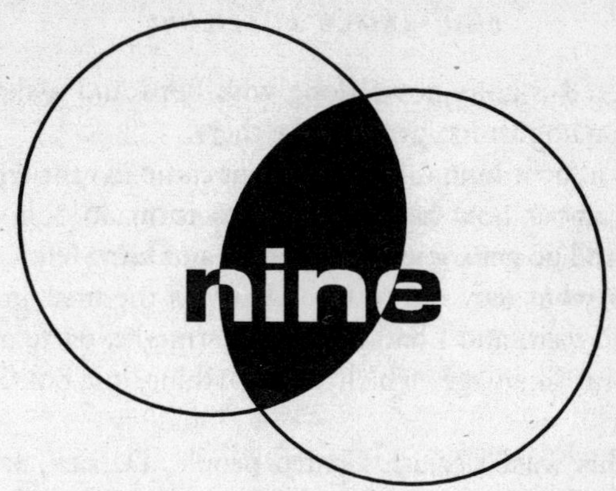

At what age do you begin to feel your dreams slipping away? And what do you do once you realize that it just isn't going to happen the way you dreamed? For a woman, the big dreams that don't stand up to reality:

1. There is no Prince Charming.

2. There are about five people in the universe who are allowed to have a "lifestyle," and the waiting list is several billion people long.

3. You won't die pretty. The most you can hope for is old age, old ugly, wrinkly age.

4. Corollary to #3: *You won't live forever.*

The men in black at Carruthers Funeral Home did a number on me. For the last few days I've been laid up in a hospital getting pumped full of fluids. Surgery to remove a slug fragment from my shoulder happened when I was brought in unconscious. The doctors have called it a flesh wound that won't leave too big a scar.

And what if they'd hit my face? What if they'd shattered a bone in my leg?

Derrick's been in to see me twice. The funeral home burned to the ground shortly after Zack Millhouse dragged me away. Whatever evidence Pops may have uncovered is gone now, along with Pops and a slew of people who just happened to be there.

It's almost funny. Derrick Trent came in ranting and raving about how he was going to form an "air cav" posse and go get some black people and hang 'em out to dry for what they did to me. That was the first time he came to visit, and I had to set him straight, particularly about his language, which was anything but politically correct.

"This wasn't South Centro people, Derrick. It was organized and executed by outsiders, outsiders with a lot of money to burn and helicopters to help them burn it."

"Jenny, there are some really rich mothers that have made a fortune in the zone." He went on to name several prominent black citizens of greater LA County.

"Relax, Zorro. These were white people. They all acted like, even moved like they had military training. And they were looking for me."

"You said they took out everybody there."

"They did. Only because they were there. They weren't the targets. I was."

"Then how'd they know you were in the zone?"

"Any number of ways. Whoever's behind it could have been watching me. Easy enough to set up aerial surveillance. Or, they could have tapped in on my conversation with Zack. He may have mentioned where we were headed. They simply waited until I was there to come after me."

"I don't know, Jen. It sounds a bit over the top."

"Think about it. Where else could you mount that kind of operation and be certain that there'd be no police presence to mess things up? They would have known that I couldn't be hooked into the office to call for help. There's no wireless coverage in the zone.

"And what would you have done if I'd never come back? The posse idea is flattering, but nobody would have gone for it. Especially if my body turned up bullet-ridden and butt-fucked on some viaduct of the Hollywood Freeway."

"Then why? Tell me that! Why?"

"Riva Barnes. Susan Bentsen. Part of the motive has to be money. Big money, as in the whole megillah."

"Speaking of which, Jeremy Bentsen has completely clammed up. No cooperation whatsoever. It's like he wants to bury the old hag, collect the insurance, and hey, baby, life goes on."

"Any clue as to why the baby killer was there?"

"Who?"

"Erasmus Trainor. The coward who killed Ada Quinn for the hell of it."

"Waters Industries Security is all-pervasive, it seems."

"Even for outside legal counsel?"

"Probably came with the retainer."

"Hmm. Then one other question."

"Yeah?"

"Was he there when you got there?"

It wasn't until his second visit that I told Detective Trent about Freddie Barnes. Barnes had to be regarded as a suspect, at least until proven otherwise.

"He's a mountain man, Derrick. He knows guns. He diddled his sister at least once that he would admit to."

"And?"

"And he's a capable."

"That guy? Capable of what?"

"Very funny. Remember how Riva died. No visible cause of death."

"So what was Susan Bentsen? Target practice?"

"Beats me. What was Eddie Reynolds?"

"Are you suggesting that we have a serial killer here?"

Be careful. Don't let him know too much.

"I don't know. We still don't have a motive."

"And unless Freddie Barnes has some rich friends who don't mind funky mountain men, we don't have a motive for the make-believe SWAT team that almost took you down in South Centro."

"Chill, Derrick. That's why I make the big bucks."

"We make the big bucks. On this one."

I can see it in his mind, that image of the two of us together on the French Riviera, on a motor sailor making sure not to spill red wine on the teak.

It's nice that one of us still has that kind of dream, Derrick. As for me—there is no Prince Charming.

The young doctor with nothing on his mind but a slew of patients and a girlfriend that he didn't see enough of came to see me on the third day. He had an intern in tow.

"I'd like to talk to you, Ms. Sixa."

"Sure. Not like I'm going anywhere."

The doctor. Not bad-looking. Wants to specialize in infectious diseases. Wants to save the world. He pulls up a chair and sits. The intern, smirking at me, hands him a chart.

Suddenly I don't want to see what's on their minds.

"The Centers for Disease Control in Atlanta have special monitoring protocols in place for telepaths," Dr. Nicholson begins. "Particularly for piggybackers."

"I'm a former piggybacker."

The doctor is looking at me intently. The distinction doesn't matter to him. "Former, you say?"

"Former. I now work with the LAPD homicide unit."

The good doctor finds this surprising. "Doing what?"

"I'm a telepath. I help identify suspects based upon the last thoughts of the victims."

"Really. But that requires a scale of capability no piggybacker has."

"Right." *Heaven.*

"But if you had that much telepathic capability, why did you piggyback?"

One of the unanswered questions of my life. What really happened that night? Parts of it I remember, parts I can't believe. "It was a long time ago." *Something lurks there, hiding under Heaven's phony clouds in memories I'd rather forget. A snippet from a fifteen-year-old's growing pains. The very baddest thing.*

"And why homicide?" the doctor says under his breath.

"Excuse me?"

"Sorry. Your history is a bit unusual. The reason for this conference is that we did some additional tests." This statement lays there and floats slowly to the floor of its own volition. He waits briefly for a reaction, a question. I say nothing.

Dr. Nicholson clears his throat. "Um, before I get

into the technical aspects, do you understand the biological basis for your, er, abilities?"

"Neurotransmitters in the brain. I can somehow read them."

"Right. But do you know why?"

I shake my head.

"Your ability, as far as we have been able to determine, is based upon a genetic polymorphism that alters a single amino acid in what's called a prion protein, or PrP. A polymorphism is a slight alteration in the nucleotide sequence of a specific gene; such variability is sometimes called an allele.

"So-called normal prion proteins are anchored to the surfaces of nerve cells. The prion proteins in telepaths are less able to adhere to nerve cell membranes. This, we think, produces a profound increase in the electrical activity of nerve cells, particularly in your brain. This heightened electrical activity in some way enhances your receptivity to neurotransmitter activity in other people in ways that we don't understand. Okay so far?"

"Yeah, I guess."

"Okay. Unfortunately, prion proteins are very unusual chemicals. Certain abnormal forms of the protein in sheep, for example, cause a disease known as scrapie. In humans, certain prion proteins cause relatively rare brain disorders, such as something called spongiform encephalopathy. Worse, there is no infectious agent that we have been able to identify, other than the protein itself."

"So you're saying that I have some sort of disease because I'm a telepath?"

"It's not that simple. You are a telepath because you have a genetic variation that produces a peculiar form of

PrP. Laboratory tests indicate that the presence of the disease-causing PrP in someone's system somehow converts your manufactured PrP into the pathogenic kind. In the case of piggybackers, the intense electrical activity in the brain during a session appears to trigger the changeover from telepathic PrP to pathogenic PrP spontaneously."

"But I haven't piggybacked in ten years!"

"True, and you haven't developed spongiform encephalopathy either. But there is evidence of pathogenic PrP molecules in your brain from your time as a piggybacker. And we think that normal telepathy slowly increases the levels of pathogenic PrP in your brain."

"What happens to piggybackers with this?"

"Well piggybacking is a much more intense telepathic episode because it involves actual mind sharing. Once enough pathogenic PrP is created, it converts the rest of the brain's PrP into the pathogenic variety of the molecule. This substance then attacks the brain, leading to rapid degeneration of tissue and, eventually, death. Peggybackers reach the threshold relatively quickly, usually within five years or so. For plain old telepaths, our models suggest the process may take much longer, but we don't know how long."

The intern smiles at me. It is not a pleasant experience. "So, Ms. Sixa, we just need to ask you some personal questions to complete the workup on this." The intern opens an autopad to begin taking notes.

"You say that you stopped piggybacking, when?"

"Ten years ago."

He makes a note on his autopad. "How long did you actually practice piggybacking?"

"Two, three years." My voice is a hoarse whisper.

"And would you say you were a, uh, typical piggybacker?"

The question is phrased to be innocuous, but they are both looking at me intently. The word "typical" by itself says nothing but implies much.

Typical piggybacker. The fourth pull on the trigger, ten years later.

"I made lots of money at it, if that's what you mean."

The good doctor and the intern exchange looks. As if I've said something significant. Which I have.

Dr. Nicholson clears his throat. "There are ways we can help you, you know."

"Yeah? How?"

"You've heard of Masque, haven't you?"

"Of course."

"We can prescribe an analogue that suppresses your reception much the way Masquc suppresses the broadcasting. That limits the electrical activity in your head. Slows down the process. It's called Sytogene."

"You mean it blocks my telepathy."

"That's correct."

"And how often should I suppress it?" *How low do I have to go?*

Again the looks.

"Our models are not good at prediction. Too many unknowns, too much variability."

But I see it in his head.

<three years as a piggybacker. ten years as a telepath. she's got to be close to the edge.>

I nod. The intern and doctor turn and walk to the door, both making stylus notes on their autopads. One stray throught from the intern—

<*. . . wonder if she still piggybacks?*>

And his pulse rate quickens. My notions of original sin are still intact.

Derrick Trent slips into my room later while I'm trying to sleep.

"Jen?" he says quietly, tenderly.

"I'm awake. Stop whispering."

"I just wanted to see how you were doing."

I just look a him. Ten years ago, stepping between me and Demarche, taking a punch, the gates already open, barbarians flooding into my mind.

"Not too good if the doctors are right."

He looks at his shoes. <*i have money. i could take care of you.*>

"Take care of me how, Derrick?"

"I . . . I'm not sure."

He's lying. He knows.

"Nicholson asked me something interesting."

Derrick looks up. "Really?"

"He wondered why I'd gotten into investigating homicides."

I'd needed protection from Demarche. Derrick was there every step of the way, helping me get settled, pulling me into his circle, pushing me to test my new abilities. I didn't just develop a taste for the work. I developed an appetite for going into crime scenes, for carrying a gun.

For protecting myself and thanking God that some poor slob lying in a pool of their own waste products and blood wasn't me.

"You do good work, Jen" is his feeble reply.

"Yeah." At first he'd kept his distance from my work with the department. Didn't want to show favoritism, even though he'd made whispered introductions to all the right people. In the early years I caught a lot of thoughts from other people about being "Trent's girl," but gradually the paydays erased the notion that such considerations were important. Then more and more he and I were working together, until I was his "girl." Untouchable, even though he'd wanted me all these years, possessed by him only because he became my sole partner within the police department. I took other cases, of course, girl's gotta work. So did Derrick. We'd risen together, our professional lives intertwined.

As for that night in Heaven, I don't know whether to thank him or not.

I was released today. My left arm is still in a sling, and thank God it's not my shooting hand that's bound up in neoprene. (I can still smack a derelict fifty feet into a stiff breeze, one-armed or not. It's all in the wrist.) There is a cop in a marked p-car following me because Derrick insisted. In fact he wanted to take me home himself, and I could see him thinking that he had a supply of Masque, that maybe he'd get lucky and convince me to let him stay.

I leave the protective surveillance at the front door to my apartment building, this place where I'm so privileged to stay. I wave to the AI door thing. It's not a real good model like Deeds, just something to recognize the people who should be there and people who shouldn't, and just enough firepower to repel boarders, so to speak. And up the elevators, up to the twenty-third floor, always wondering why I have to live on an age that's now tantalizingly out of reach, gone forever.

When it comes the panic is swift, cresting into an emotional wavelet in a hurry. I get out on my floor, and something is wrong. There's this scent in the air, like a dead animal, faint, because the air-exchangers are efficient.

There's something wrong with my door, too. Bent inward, half off the hinges. It's impolite to jack in when people are around, but there's nobody, so the contacts go into my neck, and in my head I'm dialing into Didi, wherever she is, whatever she does when she's not at the office being efficient.

<yeahboss.> There, comforting in my head.

<get LAPD on the horn. get the officer who tailed me up to my apartment right now.>

<. . . wrong?>

<break-in.>

<. . . taken? anything?>

<don't know. not inside yet.>

I'm thinking that whoever did this can't be inside, but no, I'm not willing to bet my life that I'm right. I wonder if Zack recovered my pistol. I should've seduced the uniform downstairs so I'd be safe.

<called it in straight to 911. told them.>

<what'd they say?>

<nothing. said okay, they were on it.>

<derrick?>

<not responding to my page yet.>

I realize that the elevator has left on its ubiquitous rounds. I'm effectively trapped here, 'less I care to run down twenty-something flights of stairs.

The elevator chings. They came back . . .

But it's the uniformed officer from his little p-car. Gun still in the holster.

"I got a call."

And damn him, he's thinking that maybe I liked him and wanted to jump his bones.

"My door . . ." I say, pointing. I feel stupid having to address the obvious evidence of a crime.

"Oh." He's not even good-looking, certainly not smart if he just now, you know, got it.

The patrolman pushes the door. It swings in easily. Should've gone for the electronic bank vault locks, the kind where a couple of inches of steel beam slides into the wall when the lock is engaged.

We walk in more or less together.

My place is ransacked, heavy malicious damage because I don't keep much in it.

And that smell. Man smell, old and ripe, reminiscent of real die-for-a-bath corruption.

Freddie Barnes's smell, I think to myself. Yeah.

The stink holds his vintage.

Derrick is raving about coming over to get me himself, but there isn't anything he can do. An APB on Freddie Barnes is a done deal; I've had enough of cops with their minds on their guns, if you know what I mean. Didi invites me over to her place and I greedily accept, although the thought hits me that don't have a clue as to where Deeds lives. I've heard that AI's live in these little capsules so small you can't stand up in them, an idea imported from Japan for cut-rate living. But Deeds won't put a choke hold on me in the shower, Deeds won't have a thought in her head that I can access. Perhaps I am simply tired of people, perhaps it's time to be a little bit of a robot and forget humanity.

The cab drops me at the "bin farm" which is in an industrial area, near a railyard. The lobby is incongruously neat and tidy, with a fake fireplace and a real wood desk, like an old hotel. The AI at the desk is a bit clunky. He's an obvious bolt on, sort of pot luck from the cyber reject bin.

I give him Didi's name, and he calls her "bin." There is no small talk, no bedside manner, just a task accessing a subroutine executing instructions. I wait nervously until Deeds comes out, dressed casually (I guess) in jeans pressed to razor-sharp creases and a T-shirt.

"Hi, boss."

Didi gives me a hug, an honest-to-God-girl-on-girl-needing-reassurance hug, something we never did before. I'm actually touched, and the emotion of the last few days wells up hot and bitter and angry, capped with sadness that my best friend in all the world is a machine, a fucking machine more content with her life than I am with mine, a machine whose home address I didn't know, whose house I'd never visited.

"It's a little cramped. Maybe we should rent you a bin."

She's leading me back out of the "hotel" facade, into the railyard with the dirt and the grime and the locomotives. It looks like a stack of coffins, gleaming in the moonlight, silver coffins without the bothersome dirt of humanity, without a single blemish of individuality.

The stack is honeycombed with passages and ladders, Didi is about two flights up the hard way.

"This is real . . . er, homey, Deeds."

"It isn't much. But it's home."

We are sitting on her bed, sitting because it's impossible to stand, and there are no chairs. Just a terminal, a television, and a bed. The closeness would bother me if I weren't so spooked.

"So which bed is mine?" I ask her, grinning.

"You sure you don't want to rent one for the night?"

Eeeeesh. By myself? I don't think so.

"Unless you don't want company."

"Uh-uh, boss. I gotta take care of you."

"Not really. I'm . . . a big girl." I almost said *human.*

"Sure I do. Without you I'd need a new boss."

Deeds, Deeds. Only a machine could be so loyal.

Sleeping with someone, something close, close enough to touch, is a new experience. AI's are human from just below the skin out, human with real features and hair. It's actually nice, listening to the subtle whine of the servomotors as Didi periodically adjusts to prevent the hydraulics from freezing up. I know Didi doesn't need to sleep. AI's only need to relax for a few hours while the diagnostics run. But she closes her eyes, even throws in a loud snore until I punch her in her kidneys and she giggles.

"Just don't fake a fart, Deeds."

"I can, you know."

"I'll bet you can whistle a Brahms Lullaby through your ass."

She giggles again, but when I start to say something she shushes me, saying that I need sleep.

And I do, I need to forget the world and remember a friend.

I don't sleep well, usually, because asleep I'm

defenseless against other people's thoughts and particularly their nightmares. It's usually worst when I'm working on a grisly case, the intersection of my phobias and random thought most damaging when I lay my head down.

But not tonight. Sleep, for once, comes easily.

Officer Bob shouts at my father to keep moving. I'm trying to peer over the edge of the boardwalk, staring at the form hidden by a blanket lying in the sand. Officer Bob pulls me back as my father yells at him to keep his nigger hands off his daughter. Officer Bob takes the insult, holds me back away from the edge of the boardwalk, holds me as I begin to shake. For in my dream, the BAD THING is a body, a body wrapped in a coverlette, a body lying cold in the sand while men wonder . . .

It's Riva's body, it's Genevive's body, it's Marie Folcoup's body lying sightless on the sand. And Officer Bob comforts me, holds me like a father, because I'm crying, because I'm hysterical. Because Officer Bob thinks I know something about the bad thing that I Should Not Know.

The next day at the office there is nothing different between myself and Didi, except perhaps a different level of warmth from her, a more concerned look in her lifelike eyes. Perhaps I have anthropomorphized a sophisticated machine, I don't know.

Quickly, without concentrating, I ask Didi to make the following appointments.

1. Phillip VanMeer, CEO, Celludyne. Possible Waters Industries connection.

2. Jeremy Bentsen, outside legal counsel for Waters Industries and recent widower via homicide.

3. Richard Waters, scion of Waters Industries.

4. Derrick Trent, LAPD homicide detective.

I tell Didi the order doesn't matter. Neither does the day or the time. I ask for at least an hour from each person on the list, and after thinking about it, I add the following items for consideration:

5. The Barneses. Did they know anything about Freddie's talents?

6. Zack Millhouse. At least to thank him for saving my ass. Maybe he has a different take on this mess.

7. Dr. Nicholson. I need to know more about the effects of the pills he gave me.

I try not to think about the last one.

After Didi has been turned loose on the phones, I pull out the crinkled construction paper with my crayoned diagrams. Let's try something new.

Violent crimes is the first heading.

Eddie Reynolds, Guard at the Icehouse
Susan Bentsen, Jeremy Bentsen's Wife
"Pops" Carruthers, Carruthers Funeral Home
Jenny Sixa, Telepathic Consultant

One of my first lists was the victims, myself, and concerned parties. That list:

Riva Barnes
Genevive Wilkerson
Marie Folcoup

Jenny Sixa
Mr. Right

Then there was:

Richard Waters
Arnold Waters
Jeremy Bentsen

And finally, the circle with Waters Industries in the center, with the rest of the paper blacked out by my crayon.

Phew. Okay. Let's start with the obvious. Didi has to do all the comparisons between Riva and the other Mr. Right victims using her Records Autopsy. Then Deeds has to flesh out the Waters Industries circle to summarize her voluminous notes.

Now, are the lists and the diagrams complete? Let's see. Violent crimes—I need to add one.

Eddie Reynolds, Guard at the Icehouse
Susan Bentsen, Jeremy Bentsen's Wife
"Pops" Carruthers, Carruthers Funeral home
Jenny Sixa, Telepath Consultant
Ada Quinn, Consultant to JS

On the Waters Industries people list from the initial meeting, I also must add one:

Richard Waters
Arnold Waters
Jeremy Bentsen
Erasmus Trainor

VanMeer is an unknown. Suspicious, because of his reaction to the Riva Barnes question, but still an unknown. Therefore, I can't add him yet. Looking at this, isn't it interesting that the only sure connection between the "violent crimes" list and the Waters Industries list is Ada Quinn and Erasmus Trainor. Trainor is the one person that I know is guilty.

Trainor kills in cold blood.

Trainor was there before Susan Bentsen's body was cold.

Trainor has military training according to the LAPD summaries on Waters Industries.

The only connection between Waters Industries and the icehouse besides Riva Barnes's body is the violent death of the security guard and Susan Bentsen. Both killed the same way.

Trainor was there before Susan Bentsen's body was cold.

Could Waters Industries, in the person of Erasmus Trainor, have mounted the attack on Carruthers Funeral Home? Sure. The hardest part probably was deciding which slush fund to draw down.

Does that imply that someone else on the WI list is implicated in what's going on?

Susan Bentsen. Riva Barnes. Erasmus Trainor. Richard Waters. Arnold Waters.

Masque.

Compared to Waters Industries, Celludyne Manufacturing, Inc., is a dump. Nondescript building in a lousy part of downtown LA. A purposefully decrepit and anonymous exterior facade, drab interior painted war surplus green with tacky brown indoor-outdoor carpet.

More interesting is Phillip VanMeer's reluctance to see me. Didi had to ask him if he preferred a visit from LAPD at his house. VanMeer quickly said no. So here I am.

Phillip VanMeer is a tall, gaunt Dutchman, with steel grey hair and a rapid step. He looks like a scientist-cum-businessman capable of running a laboratory or a board meeting. He smokes rapidly and impulsively, oblivious to the disgruntled looks he gets from his employees. He leads me back past the reception area into a plain office with steel furniture and plaques on the wall. This is the first meeting that I've taken with Nicholson's tablets dulling my senses. VanMeer is a wild card and seems an innocuous place to try it out.

"You asked for a meeting about Riva Barnes. I told you that I don't know a Riva Barnes," he begins, and his voice sounds like it belongs to someone else, perhaps a baritone.

"As my secretary explained . . ." It's frustrating, not being able to read his thoughts . . .

He waves me off. "No need to go through all of that. So here we are. Do you take coffee?"

"No, no thank you."

He says nothing as if he's completed his obligations to small talk. I feel the weight of a busy man who really prefers not to be bothered pressing in from all sides.

"Perhaps we should begin with a brief overview of Celludyne," I prompt.

"What would you like to know?"

"The basics . . . I know that you started the company twenty-five years ago when you were a researcher at

Stanford . . ." From Didi's manual research on the company via the Pacific Stock Exchange.

"How much do you know about microbiology?"

"Not very much."

"Let's begin with a brief overview of the field. In the mid-1990s scientists began experimenting with controlling specific genes in the body. Genes are the basic elements of cellular DNA that make us blond, for example, or blue-eyed.

"The first experiments were admittedly primitive, even though there was tremendous hope that therapeutic tools could be developed."

"Therapeutic in what way?"

VanMeer leans back in his chair. "Like killing off cells that aren't behaving normally, such as cancer cells."

"And?"

VanMeer smiled. "We're getting ahead of ourselves. The technique was to create receptors, chemicals that react to signals from the body's own chemistry to activate or deactivate a specific gene, which in turn controls a specific cellular function. Once you manufactured the receptor, you introduced a particular chemical designed to interact with the receptor to turn the genes on or off. It's actually not that simple, but I'll explain the details in a minute."

"So what happened to this research?"

"A number of problems both in and outside of the laboratory. The technique was first applied to slugs, actually, and it worked fine. The problems arose in trying to transfer the work to higher level primates and, of course, humans."

"Why?"

"The human genome projects, designed to map

mankind's genetic code, were proceeding with great success, until the governments of this country and many others decided that there were things that they didn't want known about what makes us human.

"Specifically, what if things like homosexuality were traceable to some genetic condition? A condition that could be screened for at fertilization? Or even more thorny, what if everyone knew exactly what was most likely to kill them, based purely on the genetic code they have in their cells? Everyone would then have a preexisting condition, and everyone would be crying to have drugs and other therapy developed for their particular genetic predisposition."

Like PrP defects that make you telepathic . . . "Were there other problems?"

"Yes. The attempts to upgrade the work on gene receptor sites was opposed by a significant number of the scientific community. They thought it was too close to playing God. Worse, more than a few of the experiments with humans went awry with tragic consequences for the participants. And there was the inevitable jockeying by the profiteers to somehow patent work on the human genome in the hopes of claiming royalties from drugs or other future treatments developed."

This much I remember from school: "So the Biologic Codicils of 2015 were designed to control human genome work."

"And put an end to microbiological tinkering. At least that was the design. Work on receptor manipulating drugs, like FK506, all but ceased. I think they even considered taking back a few of the Nobel prizes given in the first fifteen years of the century because of the Codicils."

"This is about ten years before you started Celludyne."

"Um-hmm. Right. For ten years nobody touched gene receptor work. You couldn't publish it, you couldn't get funding for it, you couldn't become a janitor if you had specialized in this area of work. The word from on high was clear. 'Thou shalt not experiment on the human genome!' And most people, particularly the people who were the recognized experts in the field, simply had nowhere to go and nothing to do."

"It must have been terribly frustrating."

"Maddening is more like it. That's where I came in. I did graduate work on a different class of receptor manipulating drugs. This was a class not covered in the Codicils, and my work was in a completely different area. However, my training allowed me to recognize the importance of my results to human genome work. One of the serendipities of physical science, I suppose, like mold on a sample turning out to be penicillin."

"How did you happen to stumble on these new drugs?"

"I was working on immuno-suppression techniques in skin grafting, an area where you really had to tiptoe around the Codicils and the various enforcement agencies that scrutinized that kind of work. By then, we academics had developed a whole jargon designed to shield suspect experiments from the prying eyes of the enforcement bureaucracy. We didn't feel we were doing anything wrong because we were not tampering with gene receptor work per se. But once you understand some things about biology and how things work, you can really get down to splitting some very, very fine hairs. I split them, did my experiments, and was shocked at the side effects."

"And that led you to start Celludyne?"

"Sort of. What really prompted me to start Celludyne was money. I needed money to pursue my work. Money is the province of the investment bankers." He stops to light a cigarette. "Now there's a bunch that won't hesitate to bend some rules for a fee."

"But your work was restricted by the Codicils."

"True, but the Codicils are largely academic rules designed to control academic research. They weren't laws, per se. They were ethical guidelines that everyone in academia had to follow."

"So with money you didn't need to follow the rules."

"Right. Not only did I not have to follow the rules, I could develop an entire industry without any competition. I could dust off and hire the best minds in the field, stick them in a lab, and let them do all the things they'd been dreaming of for ten years."

"Surely you weren't the only one who thought of this approach?"

"Surely not. But FK506 chemistry was illegal. That much was, and is, true about the Codicils. So while the others were brave enough to continue patently illegal experiments using illegal research drugs that were difficult to obtain or manufacture, only I had a new class of drugs that worked much the same way. My road was orders of magnitudes easier."

"And what have you done?"

Phillip VanMeer chuckled. "I can't tell you that. But I can tell you what the wet-eyed scientists who found a home at Celludyne were hoping to achieve twenty-five years ago."

"Go on."

"Well, the first thought was that we would develop drugs that would enhance the body's own defenses. As I said earlier, drugs that would activate specific genes that would make cancerous cells die off, for example. The human genome is quite a bit more sophisticated than that, however. Your body ultimately wants to die, sort of nature's balance against humanity using up all the resources and all the oxygen on the planet. So you could defend against, say, liver cancer, but speed up the development of, oh, lung cancer, just to use an example. Drug-induced gene therapy on humans was too upsetting of the natural balance of things inside us all.

"Then we thought about more finely tuning the notion of gene therapy. Are you familiar with the term 'genetic programing'?"

"No, although I take it it has something to do with gene therapy?"

"Not at all. It's a computer term. A genetic algorithm is a program that performs tasks and evaluates results, then changes its strategy based upon the results. It works when discrete strategies and discrete results can be measured, and discrete strategies can be mixed and matched."

"I'm not sure I understand. For example?"

"The classic example is as follows. You own a hamburger stand. You have the choice of charging really low prices or high prices. You can serve soft drinks or white wine. The genetic algorithm chooses, oh, say, high prices and white wine, observes the payoff, and then, in the next generation, or iteration, changes to high prices and soda, and so on. It makes its crossovers based upon observed results, thereby weeding out over successive generations strategies that don't work."

"But that's just trial and error."

"No, not at all. Remember, I said discrete strategies, discrete results, and the ability to mix and match. Such programs are true learning machines, as long as the parameters are discrete and the outcomes measurable. The next step that we thought about for Celludyne was incredibly sophisticated nanomanufactured machines, capable of evaluating their results and upgrading their strategies."

"But we already have these devices."

"That's true. We are all inoculated with a variety of mechanical agents that can handle for long periods of time discrete physiological problems, like hardening of the arteries. But the world gets sicker every day."

Damage. Drug resistant tuberculosis. The South Centro Zone.

"Why?"

"Mutagenic pathogens, like viruses and bacteria, seem to be leading the field. Virulent, drug resistant bacterial agents we've recognized as a problem since the late twen-cen. But some of the new viruses are completely unheralded in the history of mankind."

"I'm not sure I understand. What's the difference?"

"Viral agents are small, simple, and devilishly difficult to identify and get rid of. They may be virulent in the disease-causing sense, or they may be relatively benign."

"So we have an outbreak of new viruses?"

He drags on his cigarette. "'What we have is a number of pandemic new viral agents. You probably recall that HIV was one of the first modern pandemics of the last fifty years. Then we had other strains of that virus, some related to it, some not. Most of the HIV strains, like all viruses, are not new, per se."

"I thought they were."

"Most people do. Most viral infections in humans occur because zoonotic viruses, those that already exist in some species, make the leap to a new host. A relatively benign virus in a dog, for example, may become extremely virulent in a new environment, a new host. But ultimately, just about all the viral infections that have occurred are directly traceable to some preexisting viral agent in some other plant or animal. Most outbreaks that occur are traceable to something significant that has changed—for example, Brazilian Haantavirus was a direct result of clearing vast sections of the Amazon rain forest. The hosts that had hidden in flora and fauna there migrated and came into contact with humans. The virus leaped to humans, causing the brief but horrific pandemic in 2025."

"So what are you trying to say?"

"That there aren't new viruses, per se. Except for the fact that medical science has been seeing a lot of seemingly new viral agents without zoonotic ancestors for the past twenty years. Most of them have proven to be extremely virulent."

"Why not just develop new drugs?"

"There's a whole pharmaceutical industry that does just that. But it takes a long time to develop new drugs because it takes a long time to pin down the genetic code of a new virus. Remember, because of the Codicils of 2015, we're still using gene sequencing techniques that are thirty-five years old. And to make matters worse, most of the new viruses appear to be retroviruses. Their genetic engine is RNA, which requires that they use a living cell's DNA to replicate. RNA lacks many of the error protection codas of DNA. So such viruses tend to be hypermutable; that is they mutate rapidly because of transcription errors during the replication of viral RNA. When such a new virus infects a host, there isn't a single genome that we can pin down. Such agents appear as allelic swarms in their hosts, swarms with a wide variety in their genetic code. So you have to sequence a wide variety of similar agents and then determine what in the genetic structure makes the agent virulent. Then you have to develop a drug that blocks that virulence."

"So the Celludyne approach is what?"

A wan smile. "Develop nanomachines that have extremely sophisticated genetic algorithms. That can sense new cellular invasions and take action accordingly. Existing nanomachines handle a whole host of other physiological problems and new ones are being developed every day. You aren't likely to die of cancer. You aren't likely to die of heart disease that's not influenced by a pathogen. You are, however, likely to die of a pandemic viral agent."

"Wait a second. Wouldn't such things be incredibly risky to experiment with?"

"On humans, yes. I neglected to mention that we do all of our testing on AI's. About fifteen percent of their mass is living tissue. This living tissue has to be maintained at a higher level than their other components, because it is expensive to manufacture. Today, our primary products are for use in AI's, and AI's only."

"Must be a huge business."

"It is. But we still wonder about the holy grail.

Genetically programmed nanomanufacturing for the human body. If we achieved anywhere near the results that we get with AI's . . ."

"How well do your techniques work?"

VanMeer smiled. "Hell, the living tissue in our AI's is nearly immortal. It will live long after the machine's CPU has become hopelessly contaminated and must be recycled."

"But the life cycle of an AI's CPU is fifty years!"

"And we estimate that our synthetically maintained living tissues will last triple that."

It's nice to know that last night I slept with an immortal.

"What do you really know about Waters Industries?"

"Arnold Waters is a lousy golfer. Otherwise, not much."

"And Richard Waters?"

Slight hesitation. "The kid? Nice enough. Lacks balls. The old man is the company."

"What if I told you that Riva Barnes called you at least three times from her home?"

Short barking laugh. "Since I don't know who Riva Barnes is, it doesn't mean a thing to me."

"She's Arnold Waters's secretary. Or was. She's dead."

VanMeer shrugs. "So maybe it was to arrange a golf outing with Arnold. Who knows?"

It's a bravura performance, I think. But he knows more about Riva than he's letting on.

Why would Celludyne be connected with Riva

Barnes? Why would Genevive Wilkerson, Marie Folcoup, and all the others be connected to Riva Barnes?

Money. Celludyne. Biological miracles.

What cure would be worth this trail of bodies? *A telepath on a killing spree. A private detective who's dying.*

If it's a cure, I want it. Maybe Mr. Right wants it too.

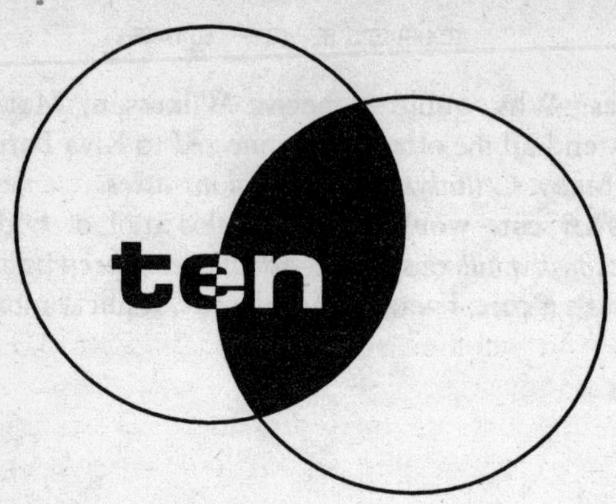

Didi informs me that my next appointment is with Jeremy Bentsen. I am not looking forward to this one, but I have to keep circling the bases in the hope that something turns up.

It's a longish ride from Celludyne to Beverly Hills. I am sure Bentsen will be using Masque, but that doesn't worry me that much. I will employ the same technique that Didi did in doing the null search on Waters Industries, look for the gaps, the body language, the obvious lies. With Bentsen I will also look for the one thing that I haven't seen anyone else experience on this case besides me—fear. *Celludyne.*

The maid, a middle-aged Spanish woman, lets me in and shows me to the same porch/foyer where Susan Bentsen's brains were blown out. I take a glass of lemonade offered from a crystal pitcher that's even better-tasting than it looks and settle down to wait.

Jeremy Bentsen looks as if he's aged ten years since that day in Arnold Waters's office. He is casually dressed in slacks and an open-necked short-sleeved shirt. The clothes are together, laundered, ironed, pressed, and coordinated. The man, however, shows obvious signs of drinking, an old, old-fashioned way to bury one's worries.

He doesn't say hello as he plops into a wicker chair. He does say:

"I'm taping this meeting. I am not prepared to answer any questions about my wife's homicide investigation. You will limit your questions to Riva Barnes and Waters Industries."

Period. I decide to go for a home run swing with the first pitch, before Bentsen has time to settle in on the mound.

"Tell me about Celludyne."

Bingo. He stares, comfortable that his thoughts aren't accessible and forgetting entirely that his body language is a shout.

"Nothing. Never heard of them." He shifts in his chair, slouching a little. A lie.

"Are they manufacturing some new microbiological miracle for Waters Industries?"

Bentsen shrugs. "I have no idea." He slouches some more, runs his fingers through his hair. A deeper, bigger lie.

"Is your wife's homicide related to Waters Industries?"

"I *told* you, no questions about Susan's death."

"Was her murder related to Celludyne?"

"Goddammit! Can't you understand simple English?"

"Does Erasmus Trainor know something about your wife's—"

"That's IT! Get the fuck out of here!"

"—Or Riva Barnes's death?"

He stands. Bentsen is a fairly big man, and he towers over me in my seat.

"Out. Now."

"Okay. I think you've given me some interesting information."

"Fuck you."

"You never will. By the way, if I tell Erasmus Trainor that you spilled your guts, what do you think he'll do?"

He's so angry that sweat pops out on his forehead. "That's why I have a tape, bitch."

"And you'll need it to satisfy Trainor? Thanks, Mr. Bentsen."

And I get the heck out of there.

I wirelessed Didi that I wanted to talk to Richard Waters right away. In person. On faith I hop a cab and direct it out to the Waters complex while I wait for Didi to get back to me. At least it gives me time to think. Celludyne may be what WI is trying so hard to hide. And I think it has a lot more behind it than tissue preservation in AI's. Lots more. But what?

<boss. richard waters isn't available. arnold waters is.>

Better than nothing. *<i'm on my way, deeds.>*

Waters Industries is serene in the early afternoon light. Once again I'm shown to the top floor with the lush carpet, once again I'm admitted into the secret warren. Arnold is standing, facing the parking lot, his desk clean, his com units silent. He's wearing a simple grey monosuit and does not seem to hear me when I walk in.

<deeds, have derrick pull a datafile on phillip vanmeer.>

Arnold rocks back and forth on his heels, humming softly to himself. I can tell he's jacked in from the slave threads leading up to the sockets in the back of his neck.

He might not have noticed me if I'd walked up to him and passed my hands over his eyes.

After five minutes he turns around, his eyes refocusing. He nods to me, reaches for a glass of water on his desk, and sits down, massaging his temples.

"Sorry. I was conferencing with Sydney." And he looks at me with those pale blue eyes, so vacant behind the wall of chemical protection, so serene, and so uncaring.

"I really wanted to see Richard. But I guess you'll have to do."

If he acknowledges the insult, he says nothing. Just those eyes, set deep in his face, staring at me.

"I wanted to know what you are going to do about Erasmus Trainor."

"Ah, yes. You still believe that he was involved in killing your friend."

"He was responsible."

Arnold Waters nods like his head is the size of Mount Rushmore teetering precariously on his neck.

"Beliefs don't mean anything in this world, Ms. Sixa. The world runs on hard cold facts. Without facts, you seem to me to be a bit long on emotion and short on ammunition."

"I asked a simple question. Do I get an answer?"

"Certainly. We are not going to do a damned thing about our head of security."

"Despite the fact that he killed Ada Quinn."

"He could kill the President of the United States for all I care. Unless someone could prove it, that is."

"What about Susan Bentsen?"

"What about her?"

"I think it likely that Trainor was involved or knows who killed her."

Arnold shrugs. "So?"

"Am I hearing you right? Are you saying that you don't care who he destroys?"

"I care about people making unsubstantiated accusations, certainly. You breathe a word of this to someone that I don't like and I'll tie you up in court for the next century."

Silence.

"Then what's it going to take?"

"Proof. Simple, incontrovertible proof. We are still a democratic society, Ms. Sixa. Innocent until proven guilty and all that. You prove beyond a reasonable doubt that what you say is true, then we will act swiftly to terminate Mr. Trainor's contract. If you get my drift."

"And are you going to help me?"

Arnold chuckles. "There you go again. We are cooperating fully with the investigation into Riva's murder. Her death is a fact, and I can't change that. But don't expect me to go tilting at windmills."

"And Richard agrees with you?"

"We have discussed this, yes."

"Hmm. Tell me about Celludyne."

The technique is common in old-fashioned lie detector tests. Change the topic quickly without allowing the subject to prepare him/herself and measure the reaction.

"Never heard of it."

"Really? They have no business dealings with Waters Industries?"

"I didn't say that. We deal with several thousand subcontractors on many of our more complicated projects. To expect me to cite chapter and verse about a company that you pulled out of a hat is absurd."

"But I think that Celludyne . . ."

". . . and Erasmus Trainor are involved in a conspiracy to murder administrative assistants and wives of corporate lawyers? Is that what you're leading up to?"

I am struck by the word games, the denial, the NIMBY notions of a man with wealth beyond imagining, a man who could at least afford to care. Here I sit in the half-assed pursuit of justice, but Riva is dead, cold and gone, and Ada, sweet Ada, whose mind was the equal of anyone's, her last thoughts glimpsed through the post-terminal fog, the wonderment of it all, summed up in one single word, a thought, a last sugary harmony of chemicals losing their impetus for living—

<damn>

but they are dead, and no matter the abstract notions of revenge, of justice, of right . . . God, Ada is dead. *And I am dying . . .*

Richard Waters enters briskly, his presence huge and unwanted as well as unexpected.

"What's going on here?" he asks, and for a moment I get a flash of déjà vu role reversal, like the son has become the parent, like this is effectively Richard's office and not his father's.

"Ms. Sixa was just entertaining me with her speculations about Riva's case. And Bentsen's wife." Arnold finishes his report and falls silent.

Richard turns to me, obviously distracted, his mind blank to me because of Nicholson's Sytogene. "Why don't you fill me in?"

"Sure. I'm wondering about . . ."

"Not now. Not here." Richard looks at his watch. "I'm tied up here until early this evening."

"Is this investigation important to you or not?"

Arnold: "Of course it's important, Ms. Sixa."

Richard frowns. "I'm rather tired of your insinuations. We didn't kill Riva Barnes."

"How about Susan Bentsen?"

Arnold: "What the hell is that supposed to mean?"

"Erasmus Trainor was there, dammit! What about it, Richard? Did your people kill Susan Bentsen?"

"This is absurd. I won't dignify that with an answer."

"Because you don't have one? Or because you don't want me to know the answers?"

"Excuse me, I have a meeting . . ." I grab his arm.

"Wait a fucking minute, Richard. Do I get my questions answered or not?"

Richard looks at my hand on his arm like it's bird poo. Resigned: "Can you make dinner?"

I hesitate. Let go of his jacket. Smooth the fabric. "That's better. Where and when?"

Richard scrawls an address on a piece of notepaper from Arnold's desk. He starts to hand it to me, then takes it back and jots something else. "This okay?"

It's the address of a restaurant, and a time, 8 PM.

"I'll see you there," I murmur, looking at the stiff milled notepaper. "Arnold Waters." As in, "From the desk of—"

As I get ready for my tête-à-tête with Waters it occurs to me that the Barnes case has too many things going against it. The fact that Riva's body turned up in South Centro effectively minimized most standard police procedures, like canvassing the area for witnesses. The official "don't give a damn" posture even missed the second homicide of the guard right there on the premises of the icehouse, another valuable lead completely botched.

At least the cleaning thing has reduced the damage in my apartment to a dull roar. It's almost passable until I go check my closet for something slinky to wear for my "date" and discover that Freddie Barnes or whoever trashed my homestead did a number on my evening gowns. One more thing for the insurance company, although even a man as bloodless as Richard Waters would get a hard-on if I appeared in the shiny strips the vandal made of my classy clothes.

This upsets me greatly. I obsess about my look, trying to get it just right for these kinds of occasions. I could go with something short and overcompensate with jewelry, maybe a translucent mini turned toward the obscene side of clear.

And no underwear. At least that would take the pressure off of being underdressed. Bare is in these days anyway. Not naked, but bare(ly) dressed is in. All the pencil-necked models love to show off how boyish their bodies are, a triangular patch of pubic hair the only badge of femininity that's noticeable.

As I dress I review the details so far. Bentsen afraid of Trainor. Arnold looking like the son and Richard looking in control. Celludyne possibly a dead end, if I can't get more information. I'm tempted to call Didi to see how the cross tabs are going between Riva's records and everything else in the universe, but I decide not to.

And of course, there's Freddie Barnes, the one-eyed jack in the deck, lurking somewhere to trump the play when it looks interesting.

There. I'm ready to face the world. Doc Nicholson's Sytogene tablets have worn off, and I briefly debate taking another one.

Something tells me not to.

La Tropique is so named because the circular layout is ringed in a massive fish tank, easily large enough to hold sharks and other exotic fish. Most women hate the place because the light filters greenish through the tank, playing havoc with carefully applied makeup. It can also be unnerving to sit in the outer ring of seats when it's feeding time.

I'm early, so I let the valet park my nondescript little p-car next to a charging stand. I don't bother giving him a tip because he's ogling the flesh beneath the clothes that aren't quite there. Thrills will have to do, young fella.

I'm expecting Richard to roll up in one of those mag-lev limousines shaped like a large dildo, and I'd like to catch a glimpse of how the other one percent lives. I also don't want to subject my tortured synapses to the discordant babble inside just yet.

The night is clear and cool, with maybe a hint of rare rain in the air. I'm watching a limousine work its way down the street when Richard Waters touches my arm, startling me.

"Where'd you come from?"

"I've been here for a while. I thought I would just

watch you from inside for a few minutes when I realized that you were standing out here waiting for me."

He's wearing a snappy double-breasted suit with a black T-shirt for hipness. The material flows over the tips of his black shoes, which are highly polished. He looks like a mogul from the past, a hip young guy who makes his credits as a creative genius who just happened to be in the right place at the right time once.

"Come." He gently takes my arm and steers me into the dining room. His attitude is a big change from this afternoon, coolly obsequious so that it makes me nervous and suspicious. He steers me to an expansive table, removed from the rabble in a plush nook sunken into the floor. A piano player sits on a raised dais in the middle of the sunken living room playing softly. All of the surrounding tables are empty and reserved.

"Are we in no-man's-land on purpose?"

He chuckles. "I usually come here with business associates. It helps to deter incidental eavesdropping."

"Old habits die hard. Of course, anybody with fifty credits' worth of electronics can hear everything that gets said."

Richard nods. "But I have them screen everyone at the door for obvious . . . devices."

We sit. The wine steward comes automatically and refills Richard's glass. He pauses to ask if I would like to imbibe as well.

"Let's see what the boy tycoon is drinking." It's a nice California Chardonnay. "Seems fine to me. Fill 'er up."

Richard is busy putting papers into a thin briefcase. He's obviously been working while waiting for me.

"What is that stuff? Been buying up third world countries?"

He actually laughs. "Something like that."

"Then how come I can't get any help on Riva's case? Or on that bastard Trainor?"

"I think we've cooperated completely with your requests. And by the way, Trainor is here."

"Where?"

"Around. Anytime I leave the office for an unsecured location I have a full security detail, which Trainor heads, at least tonight."

"Where is that murdering bastard?"

Richard looks at me. "He's around."

"Look, I don't know what kind of game you're playing out in la-la land, but that guy is a menace."

"I know."

"Then why not do something about it?"

"That's part of the reason I consented to talk to you tonight."

"You need me to work on the precise wording of his termination letter, perhaps?"

Richard sips, thinking. "Let's just say that Trainor has become a . . . problem."

"No shit, Richard. He runs around killing people who don't play by your rules. Unless he's got this really rogue version of the company policy manual I'd say it's a big damn problemo."

"Have you ever heard the expression that 'business is war'?"

"No. You ever heard the expression 'murder is illegal'?"

"Not funny. What I'm trying to say is that sometimes you need soldiers to do the dirty work."

"And Trainor is a soldier?"

"Right. And has been a loyal soldier for many years."

"Loyal to whom?"

"My father."

"Which means what?"

"Which means that he has a lot of embarrassing information that he's stockpiled over the years. Which means that he can't simply be fired."

"Which means he's a loose cannon."

Richard shrugs. "I've noticed a tendency for our Security department to go a bit over the top in the last few years. Some of the, how shall we say, excesses have been quite brutal."

"Like Ada Quinn." You chickenshit bastard. She's dead, and you make excuses.

"Like Ada Quinn."

"Why not do unto him as he did unto Ada?"

"He's got files that have to be reencrypted every so often or they go into the public nets. Or so he says."

"And you have no way of verifying this?"

"We believe that any attempt to find out will lead to immediate disclosure."

"What could be so bad that you'd keep him?"

Richard shakes his head. For the first time I notice that his inner voice has been completely silent the whole evening. Damn that Masque!

"Okay." Take a breath, Jen. Go for the jugular.

"Does any of this have anything to do with Celludyne?"

Cool stare. "Who?"

"Celludyne."

"Never heard of it."

"Then why did Jeremy Bentsen react so strongly when I asked him about it?"

"Bentsen is a fool. His wife's murder hasn't helped his faculties at all."

Pause for effect. Then—

"Is Trainor blackmailing you?"

There is a long silence as Richard turns his head to gaze at the fish tank. A grey manta glides through the green water.

"Richard?"

From far away. "Yes, Jenny."

"If he's blackmailing you or the company, I can nail him for you. But only if I know everything. Only if you release the interdict. Do you understand?"

"Trainor would know in an instant if I did that."

"There are ways around it."

"Like how?"

"Easy. A new ID with clearance into your systems. That plus a different hardware setup would do it."

"I'll have to think about it."

A familiar hand on my neck, a familiar voice; his hand caresses my hair in that possessive way men have at their most inappropriate moments. "Then I think you should put on your thinking cap," Derrick Trent says, thinking

<this guy's just a playboy asshole, Jen.>

"Detective," Richard acknowledges him, amused.

"Mind if I join you?" He's already pulling over a chair.

I crook my finger at him. Derrick leans over so that I can whisper in his ear.

"Move your hand or I'll bite it off."

He moves his hand. Richard suppresses a huge smile.

Derrick looks at Richard. I look at Derrick. Richard looks at the two of us.

"To what do I owe this pleasure, Detective Trent?" Richard the chameleon again, all phony charm.

"Nothing. Happened to be in the area. Saw the two of you. Came over to say hello."

"Hmm. I see. Lucky us."

<rich people, christ!> "I take it you were talking about the case?"

His voice has a slightly hopeful tone to it. Richard looks at me, catches the barest hint of my shrug, and decides to run with it.

"We were going to, actually." Richard's smile to me is so warm and so theatrical that it's all I can do not to laugh. Derrick reaches for a water glass—

". . . Once Jenny and I finished finalizing plans for our trip this weekend. We were thinking of Monaco."

<oh, shit!> Derrick in a sudden panic . . .

Richard reaches for my hand, caresses each of my fingers in turn. "It was Monaco, wasn't it, sweetheart?" His real smile is right there, just under the surface, and we are both struggling to keep straight faces.

"Yes, Richard honey. It was . . . Monaco." As breathy and stupidly sexy as I can muster.

Derrick, curt: "Can I talk to you a second, Ms. Sixa?" Richard turns away to hide his face.

"Sure, Detective."

He carefully removes my hand from Richard's. Hauls me to my feet. Drags me toward the front foyer.

* * *

"Have you lost your mind, Jenny?"

"What the hell are you doing here, Derrick?"

"Keeping an eye on you. Besides, um, I eat here quite a bit when I have time."

"You must have an incredibly lucrative hobby, Derrick. Most cops can't afford to drive by the place and look at the sign, much less eat here—what did you say?—quite a bit?"

"He's bad news, Jenny. He's the worst of the love 'em and leave 'em types."

"Thanks for the news flash. I'll take mad money in case I have to make my own way after I fuck his brains out in Monaco. That's right, Derrick, M-o-n-a-c-o."

"You can't do that, Jenny!"

"I can't? Did you say, can't? Maybe I'll go back in there and fuck his brains out in his limo, Derrick. Whad'ya think about that?"

<fucking piggybackers.>

I turn away suddenly furious with him. He hasn't pulled this shit in years and he knows how I feel about it. He wants to be uncomfortable? Well let's just walk right back to the table and give him an eyeful.

Richard sees me coming, Derrick in tow, but his expression is all wrong. So wrong that it slows me down.

Richard shakes his head gently, looking not at me but at Derrick Trent. "I'm afraid Ms. Sixa and I have been playing a little game at your expense, Detective. We were talking about the case, not anything else. Your Ms. Sixa hates my guts and everything I stand for, don't you, Jenny?"

My mouth opens but no sound comes out. Richard tilts his head to look at me and for a moment the disappointment is obvious. "I find that to be a pity, don't you, Detective?"

Without waiting for an answer Richard walks out of the restaurant.

Derrick and I walk out to the parking area. He speaks first to break the silence.

"I came to tell you we almost had your lover boy on ice."

"Who?"

"Freddie Barnes."

"Almost? I wasn't aware we were playing horseshoes."

"He overpowered two officers. They stumbled on him in a homeless camp."

"Overpowered, you say." I'm thinking foolishly about his smell.

"Mind-fucked them. I'm going to the captain with this. I think he qualifies as suspect number one." *<along with lover boy.>*

Silence for another step or two. "So are you going to tell me about your dinner with Richard?"

"He did tell me some interesting things about Erasmus Trainor."

"Like what?"

"Like Trainor is a nutcase who's shaking them down for money."

"Maybe that's why Trainor sees you as such a threat."

"*Moi?* I'm as sweet as key lime pie."

"Ugh. No wonder I can't get the taste of you out of my mouth."

"Keep it up and I will go to M-o-n-a-c-o with 'lover boy.' "

That shuts him up. Then:

"You know, I think we should lean on Jeremy Bentsen. Together."

"For what?"

"There's a company called Celludyne that might figure in this somehow. Bentsen went apoplectic when I asked him about it. Richard was decidedly cool. I think if we blindside Bentsen he'll tell us something significant. Call Bentsen, get an appointment to see him right now. I'll meet you there."

"Aw, Jen. It's late. Bentsen can wait until tomorrow."

"Derrick, we need to push Bentsen. He's on the edge. If he doesn't know I'm coming we might get something out of him."

"You think he knows who killed his wife?"

"I think he knows how Trainor pulled it off. He knows a few other things, too."

"Oh, and, Jen, who's VanMeer? Didi asked me to pull a datafile."

"And did you?"

"Couldn't. I'm interdicted."

"So you couldn't get any data on VanMeer?"

"There already is a datafile on him. Restricted access." He hesitates for effect, knowing that I'm curious. "Think large dollars, Jen. Large dollars without a visible means of support."

"Isn't Celludyne profitable?"

"Celludyne's his company."

"Uh-huh."

"Investigations ran him through the compiler because

things didn't quite add up. The file was never turned into an active investigation, however."

"Which makes the restricted access curious, doesn't it?"

Derrick chuckles. "Yup. See you in the Hills of Beverly."

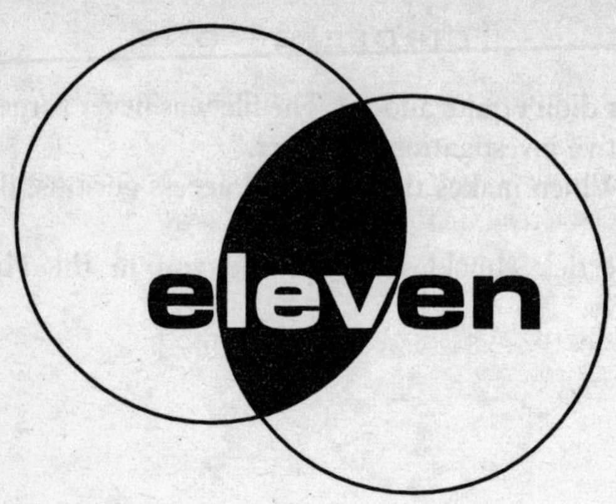

Jeremy Bentsen looks as if the dead of night has settled in on his soul. Derrick arranged it so that I could walk in unannounced minutes after he did to catch the lawyer off guard. The maid, Maria, looked at me like I was an apparition as she admitted me to the house.

<cops don't know a damned thing! so stupid.> "I don't know anything more about the murder, Detective. I thought you had something important for me, something that couldn't wait."

"We do. In fact, I believe she's on her way in, now."

<the telepath. shit.>

"Mr. Bentsen. We meet again."

<watch it! watch what you think.> "I thought I already threw you out once today."

"Tell me about Trainor."

<fucking thug killed . . .> "I don't know what you're talking *<. . . my wife>* about."

"Why don't you tell me? Detective Trent can put you under protective custody if you're afraid of him."

<as if Trainor is the real problem.> "I have nothing to say. Detective, I must ask you and Ms. Sixa to leave." *<I say one word about anything I'm a dead man.>*

"We can always take you in for questioning." Derrick smiles.

"I can also have you busted back to being a meter maid, Detective." *<they don't know anything. they're just fishing.>*

<let 'em fish.>

"Richard Waters told me something interesting about Celludyne, Jeremy."

<damn! don't react!>

"He said that Celludyne would change the world for the better."

<hah! what a crock. maybe it'll change my world.> "I wouldn't know."

"I think you do know. I think your wife was killed because of what you know. As a warning."

"So what exactly is Celludyne?" Derrick asks, and I almost will him to shut up.

"Are they cooking up something for Waters Industries?"

"I don't know anything about *<they better let me in on it.>* Celludyne! How many times do I have to tell you?" *<after all this . . .>*

"You weren't supposed to find out about it, were you, Jeremy?"

Bentsen sits in stubborn silence.

"Was Riva killed because of Celludyne?"

<an afterthought. the woman was an afterthought, i bet. i need some leverage to get them out of here! get rid of them now!> "Look, I could probably blow the whole case wide open."

"Then Riva's death was connected."

<who cares! who cares about some woman.> "I'm not saying that. I'm just saying that I . . . *<my life is in*

danger.> my life is in danger. I'm not free to discuss . . . things because *<of client privilege>* of client privilege."

Derrick: "We can protect you."

<bullshit.> "I need time to think things through."

"Your wife was a warning, wasn't she?"

<warning? hell. she was my lesson that I'd fucked up and . . .> "I don't know what to think."

Bentsen stands up, running a hand through his thinning hair.

"You're obstructing a homicide investigation, Bentsen. Don't make this any more difficult than it has to be."

<great. b-flick cop. thinks he can scare me more than they do. get a life, cop. wake up and get a life.> "Don't threaten me, Detective."

Bentsen stands and begins pacing the floor, the Spanish tiles clicking softly under his slip-ons.

"They're going to have you killed. You must know that."

"Is that so."

"You know these people. They don't share anything. You must know that."

<but I know. I know about the plans.> "They would have done something by now if that were true." *<and I'm trying to prove useful to them.>*

He's standing in the middle of the porch, right about where his wife lay after she was killed.

Derrick and I exchange a look. "So Celludyne is the key?"

<celludyne is life itself.> "I'm not going to say anything."

"It has something to do with microbiology, right? Something that prolongs life . . ."

<that ain't the half of it, bitch.>

"There's more, then? You just thought 'that ain't the half of it, bitch.' "

Bentsen looks at me with horror, as if he'd let his guard down just an inch.

"You must leave right now. Right . . ."

There is a tinkle of glass breaking, and Jeremy Bentsen stops speaking. Another tinkle, and a bright red spot wells from his chest—there is a bullet hole right between his eyes.

"Sniper! Jenny! Get down!"

Bentsen sort of rolls backward on legs made of jelly. His head slaps the floor as automatic weapons open up from the outside, suppressors making the sound pitter patter as bullets pour through the porch spraying glass.

"Shots fired! Bentsen home in Beverly Hills . . . officer needs assistance!" Derrick is jacked in now, shouting as well as thinking to get the backup rolling.

I'm crawling over to Jeremy Bentsen's body, feeling for a pulse on his wrist, his neck, anything. There is lead flying everywhere, clips full of it being emptied into the porch as Derrick tries to drag me into the house proper.

"Get off of me, Derrick!" I shake him loose, my hands on Jeremy Bentsen's, the flesh still warm, the blood starting to pool from the back of his head and his chest wounds. I'm searching for something, anything from his mind, but all I get is a fleeting thought—

<they tested it>

and the firing stops abruptly. There are sirens in the distance and Derrick is whispering to himself, probably plugged into the approaching police vehicles, trying to block the assailants' escape routes.

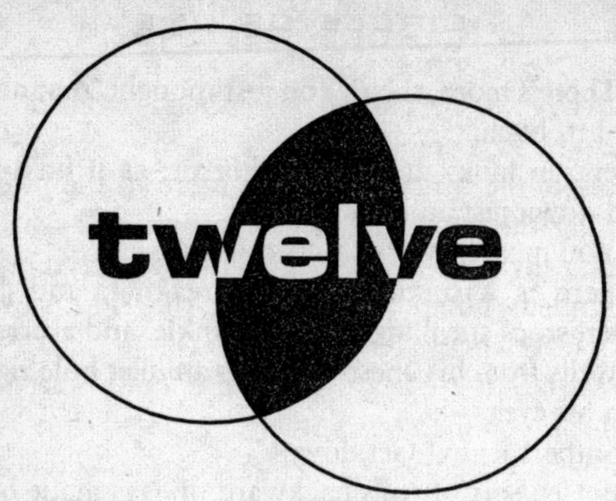

twelve

Bentsen is dead and a squad of killers is about. Of course I'm packing, and I'm going to find the nearest door to pursue the death squad, no doubt Trainor's death squad.

There is a cold familiarity of steel in my hands, the reaction so smooth and practiced that I don't know how the gun got there, and I don't know how I know that it's loaded with the safety snicked off.

There are doors to the left of the body that lead onto the lawn. The doors I came in, what was it, yesterday? Day before? When Bentsen's wife was the recipient of the bullets.

Ignoring Derrick's shouts I sprint for that door, outside into the coolish night, the silent night now that the gunfire has stopped.

Cut to the right, head for the clump of vegetation. Shots came from the right, through the window, looking now for a spot, for spent brass, for anything, even a scent that there were killers here.

A broken trail of twigs and branches indicates the path of their retreat. How far ahead are they? Far enough to get to a vehicle? Probably, although a p-car would have to be parked far enough away not to be ID'd at the scene by witnesses.

Follow the trail. Wish I ran more in the mornings. Don't let the gun hand be compromised by a branch blocking my path—effectively pushing everything aside one-handed. Where the fuck are they? Legs wobbly, head a little woozy. Ignore it.

Stealth is the enemy of speed. I must sound like a squad of commandos coming through the Mekong Delta back in the bad old days. The opening, when it appears, surprises me, I stumble into the clear, Christ! Duck damn you, down on the ground, cursing the wasted seconds until a shot whistles overhead, back into the man-made jungle that marks the end of Bentsen's property.

If it's the sniper he's probably lost me in the narrow viewfinder of his scope. That means his spotter will be looking at the grass where I lay, pulling his partner's aim down and to the right.

Roll *left* . . . just as shots kick up tufts of grass and dirt, denuded roots rich with dark soil. Too hard to pick up muzzle flash, hard to know where to look as the line of impacts tracks me down . . .

Fire a wild round into the general direction of the suppressing fire. To my knees now, running left, then cutting back to the right as fast as I can in a crouch. No muzzle flash, no thoughts drifting in from the darkness. Nothing . . .

Something knocks my gun out of my hand. Whirl on someone dressed in black, kick out at the arm, deflect his weapon as a shot whistles by . . .

No good. He swings the rifle stock around, nicking my temple, and my head explodes in pain and my knees buckle. I can feel the rifle coming down toward me, roll away, but not quite far enough, muscles twitching, almost like they're not under control anymore, the heavy plastic stock misses me, but not by much.

Kick at his groin, feeble—what's wrong with me!—my pistol under my left arm in the grass. The rifle coming back to his shoulder, awkward at close range . . .

My pistol barks first, second, game set and match as:

A car door slams, the whine of the electrics jump starting. There! Long long shot, too far for a pistol, fuck it and pull the trigger for the aggravation. Pick myself up like a drunken sailor, run on the vehicle. Recoil, legs pumping as the p-car turns on two wheels to reverse course up the street. Recoil, recoil, recoil, and a bullet smashes the back window. Run, runrunrunrunrunrun, recoil again, the car skids against the curb. I am rewarded with a spray of an automatic weapon through the busted-out back window. Down on my knees, still firing, the driver's side opens up and a body hits the pavement. The p-car wobbles to the middle of the street, accelerates.

Shoes off, it's a sprint now against the wind-up electric motor revving to put some distance between my gun and somebody's back but I have no energy for this, no e-n-e-r-g-y.

I empty the clip as I reach the black-clad body lying still on the pavement. Another clip, the p-car out of range now, and I turn to survey the damage.

From the way the body lies curled on the street I can see my entry and exit wound, back of the shoulder, out through the breastbone. Not the fatal wound, as the powder burns on the man's chest indicate. When the driver got hit, he became expendable.

Quickly I kneel down. The cavalry is arriving. I touch the man's neck, the exposed flesh still slightly warm, probing, probing, but something is wrong. There is nothing in this man's mind, as if his brain chemistry has been dead for a century. I have a fleeting thought—why would a hit man be using Masque?

Jenny

From behind me, a thunderclap that buckles my knees. My hands are still around the shooter's neck trying desperately for contact as someone else comes up behind me, rough hands lifting me to my feet, the images he's pumping into my head more obscene and deluded than anything I've ever experienced.

My knees are too weak to stand, the fatigue from my little sprint through the bushes comes rapidly over me. There is no physical smell, as if he'd washed himself in disinfectant, no mountain man's beard, no hair of any kind on his face or scalp. He's pouring his filth into a crack in my head as he lifts me, helpless to resist, and gently twists the gun from my hand.

Freddie Barnes has found me. He is taking me to a place where he can finish me off. His way. And I'm too weak to resist.

Riva is a demanding bitch in bed. She ridicules Freddie, telling him that if he can't get it up for his sister, how can he possibly satisfy some other woman? She likes to chain him up and beat the crap out of him.

"Not in my head, Freddie. I want it here. It's wet and it's ready. C'mon . . . wimp! Wimp! C'mon,

Freddie, even a wimp like you can get it hard for me . . . c'mon . . ."

The building is deserted, as near as I can tell somewhere near the South Centro Zone. The assault on my head is nonstop, and I am chained to a grate, spread-eagled and buck naked while Freddie prances around alternately jabbering and fondling the dead girl next to me. She is lying atop a long coffinlike box with fresh dirt clinging to its sides—dirty clothes pushed aside for a view of her vagina and a single translucent pearl of semen clinging to her mons.

He prepared her with rubbing alcohol, a crescent of clean puckered white skin that extends just beyond her pubis and a third of the way down her thighs. Her neck is twisted at an absurd angle, her eyes, open, stare at me framed by stringy black hair . . .

Riva Barnes with a leathery strand of whip in her mouth, chewing it, Freddie facedown with angry welts around his buttocks and back, a scene so bizarre that it strains credibility . . .

Freddie kisses the dead girl, twisting his neck so that his lips can meet hers, rubbing his crotch, pulling down his zipper . . .

Riva is impaled on him, riding him, ecstasy twisting her face into something cruel and tender, Freddie's point of view is all penis, sliding in and out, growing monstrous with blue veins.

The real thing is quite a bit less impressive. He masturbates over the dead girl, fingers sliding a desperate rhythm over his organ until he sweeps her aside, off the coffin, and pries the lid open.

He dug up Riva's body.

Freddie sobs, wounded by the sight of her and the

stench of formaldehyde, his hand reaches down between her legs.

"I loved her!" he wails, and suddenly his morning mouth is spraying my face with spittle.

I stare clear-eyed at him and I am rewarded with a cinema vérité view of Freddie taking Riva in the ass.

"I loved her!" he wails, and he kisses me quickly, his tongue sliding between my teeth before I can clamp my mouth shut. There is rubbing alcohol on his face, on his scalp. His dick brushes my bare leg.

He shifts position, now kneeling between my legs. He squeezes a breast roughly, paws my inner thigh in a clumsy imitation of passion. My legs twitch involuntarily, trying to close against the handcuffs chafing my ankles.

"I'm not dead yet, Freddie," I say softly.

Everything stops. "What's that supposed to mean?"

"Your girlfriend. You fucked her dry, did you? I bet you like 'em cold, you asshole."

He glances at the dark-haired girl with the neck problem.

"I . . . I didn't . . ."

"Sure. Like she would let a freak like you near her? Uh-uh. Not unless she was beyond having a choice."

"No. No! You don't understand!"

I let my gaze drift down. "Shit, Freddie. Go ahead

and rape me. With that little thing you got, I probably won't feel it."

He slaps me then. "Yeah, Freddie. Just like Riva used to do to you!"

He slaps me again, harder this time. I taste blood in my mouth.

Now wouldn't be a bad time for the cavalry.

<thirty seconds max, boss.>

Freddie pulls back, surprised at Didi so close in my head.

"Oh, did I forget to tell you?" I look at him sweetly as sirens become audible. They're getting louder. There are a lot of them.

Freddie leans in, snarling.

"You just better find whoever did this to my sister."

And then he's gone.

Derrick Trent is the first to come through the door and see me in all my glory. In my anger, in my fear, in my humiliation, I focus all of my ability on him, waiting to tear him apart for the slightest little slip of thought, of focus on my sex, on my nakedness. Here I am, spread open for him in a terrible parody of willingness, about to lose my famous grip on it all, right here, right now.

He turns away. He didn't look, didn't think. For all I know he was just an apparition standing there in the doorway.

A female officer comes in, a thickset black woman, and I resent having fallen into the ultimate trap of being a female in need of assistance, of being too frail for the husky demands of the world. For needing Derrick to be understanding.

I hate it all. Just as I long to be alone, I long to not need anyone.

Ever.

Later when I am dressed, Derrick gently probes me about Fast Freddie, grave robber.

His last words to me, imploring me to find who killed his "beloved" sister, will stay with me. They might imply innocence, or denial. He may not have killed the other one, just fucked her. Fast Freddie can fend for himself with the law.

Didi bailed me out of this jam. Freddie left me jacked in, and Didi locked my implant signal into a Global Positioning System satellite somewhere overhead. Took the GPS plot and slapped it on a grid of the city, told the police where I was. And did it all by me calling her name in my head when I came to, because Freddie would have known the play if I'd had to do any thinking about it.

"Jenny." Derrick says my name gently, a tone that I do not like. I nod, as in, continue.

"You should think about getting out of this one, Jen."

"Why?" as if the answer isn't obvious.

"Because you're taking too many chances. Because you're sick. There was no reason to go after the hitters at Bentsen's house. My own people might have killed you if they'd rolled up at the wrong time."

"What about the two I nailed? Does that suggest that I'm ill?" But of course it does. Because I feel like hell.

"That's my other point. We think we can tie them into Trainor. That would tie Trainor into Susan Bentsen's killing as well, if we stretch the truth a little bit. Probably puts Trainor into the thick of it with Riva Barnes, as well."

"And Freddie?"

Derrick sighs. "He's a problem, true. But he could just be some nut from a fucked-up family."

With a thing for his sister. Or was it the other way around?

And then there's Celludyne. And Ada.

"I can't just walk away. You know that, Detective." *If it is Celludyne, if it is a miracle, then I need one right about now.*

He's taken aback by me calling him that. I haven't called him a dick since the first twenty seconds of our professional relationship. I just feel a need to send him packing after what he's seen and hasn't addressed.

He nods, lighting up a cigarette. I take the lit one from his hand and turn away to the grey Los Angeles night without thanking him or saying anything more. He flares another match behind me, and says softly that they have a dragnet out for one Freddie Barnes; men armed with tranquilizer guns with darts filled with Sytogene. Shit.

They expect to pick him up soon.

And if I find him first, God rest his tortured soul, I will make him regret that he has a cock.

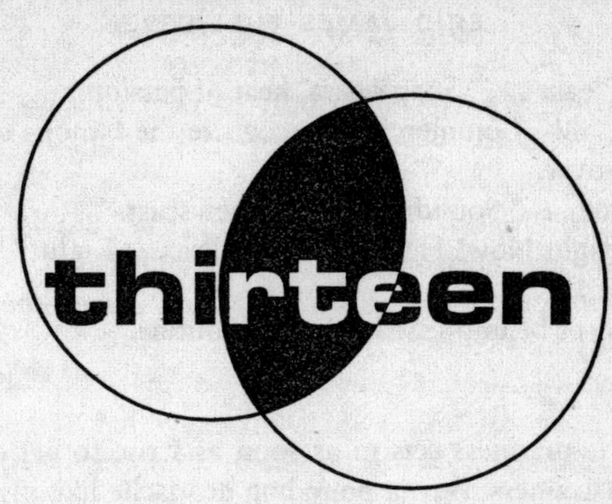

thirteen

The morning arrives too quickly by about half a day. I'm lying in bed, tuned out to everything, not even jacked in because I know Didi will call me from the office and actually want me to think.

Well the hell with that. At eleven I'm turning over for the third time, just about to really get decadent with the z's, when the lights begin blinking.

Go away. I pull the pillow over my head.

Random appliances begin turning on and off. The television clicks on, runs through the channels, blasts the volume on the rock video channel. And yes, the phone is ringing and it is loud.

Didi does this when she can't reach me in my head. She calls it "appliance revenge." The message is to please call and the craziness will stop. She's quite good at creating chaos in here, overrevving the blender in the kitchen is a new one. I've been thinking about getting secured wiring, you know the kind the Pentagon uses to shield against Electro Magnetic Pulse. Didi's getting desperate—one of her favorite tricks is to slam the teevee through the channels at high volume so that the words create the appropriate message—

"Please . . ." Soap opera, heat of passion.

"Call!" Commercial, I recognize the famous actor's voice-over.

"me . . ." Sound bite from a newscast.

"Right Now! Here on . . . the Price is Right!" Game show.

Don't be impressed. It's a subroutine.

The dizziness sets in as soon as I rise to get out of bed. Dizziness, then a pounding headache like my head is caught in a vise. The pain is so intense that I whimper a little because I've never felt anything like it. Lying back down doesn't help, in fact shifting my center of gravity only makes the pain move around, like my head is full of corrosive piss with a massive throbbing turd floating at the epicenter.

Two minutes of this and I'm ready to cut my wrists. I think of Sytogene, of PrP, bad things, bad things that I don't want to think about. I wonder if this is how it begins.

I reach for Nicholson's vial and hesitate. What if Sytogene makes the pain go away?

Then I'd know.

A blast of pressure on my temples makes me compromise. Couple of aspirins, maybe a slightly stronger painkiller on top of them, and Sytogene. I wonder how many brain cells I've destroyed by moving around to get the meds together along with a glass of water.

After chugging this rather surly morning cocktail it's all I can do to lie back down. For a second. Because if Didi starts up with the appliance shit again I'll jump out the window and enjoy the fucking trip down.

I jack in.

<boss, this is a loop for when you jack in. just got a warehouse receipt from a company called deltec inc. for some equipment that's sitting in a condo on the boulevard. can't get anything from the nets on them. looks like hot stuff from the manifest . . . boss, this is a loop for when you . . .>

Richard. He came through after all.

Didi will hightail it over to the apartment to set up the stuff. I'll need to lose any tails that are on me. Trainor is clearly monitoring everything that he can. He must be tapped into the public com systems. That's why his killers were on Masque last night.

He knew that I'd be there. That's the way Didi figures it.

Erasmus Trainor is about to take a hit, or so I hope.

The pain in my head subsides. Time to move.

It's close to five in the afternoon when the cab drops me at the Waters Industries complex. A rare thunderstorm threatens, the sky is black. At least the prospect of rain has cooled the city. The rain will wash some of the crap out of the atmosphere.

Richard is waiting for me outside his father's office. I make a mental note to have him show me his office one of these days simply because it seems as if he doesn't have one.

"Jenny." He greets me warmly, or so I imagine. His mind is closed to me because of the Sytogene.

"Richard."

"You wanted to see me."

"Yes, yes I did. I think we should talk."

"About Riva."

I nod. *But not here.*

"But not here."

I nod again. Money must make people perceptive. If so, I should therefore be rich.

"Do I need my security team?" Richard Waters is beaming.

"Nope. You're ultra safe with me."

"Hmm. That's a pity."

With that we leave the compound.

There are places in Los Angeles where it is possible to be alone. Not just alone, but away from the potential of surveillance of any kind short of the NSA sticking a chip up your you know what.

"We found the files, thanks to your little gift." Didi was right. The computer equipment he'd sent was hot stuff.

"I should have that ID shut down then?"

"Yup. Nothing more to be done on my end."

"How can you be so sure?"

"Trainor does have files that must be reencrypted periodically. Lots of safeguards around his personal stuff. We used a virus to get in."

Richard shakes his head. "We've got the best protection that money can buy against that kind of trick."

"I know that. The prototype of this one is very similar to the way a biological virus works. Small enough to be unnoticed by the immune system, it just sits there and grows embedded inside the file code. Gradually takes over the code itself. Makes the program do its own bidding."

"And then?"

I shrug. "Poof! No more records." This is Didi's thing. She explained to me that very few things turn on an AI like hacking software. So clear those registers, sweetheart. Maybe I'll get them to juice the voltage at the bin farm.

"How long before this happens? I mean, erasure of the files."

"Already history. If Trainor checks, he won't see anything amiss. But nothing intelligible can get out of the WI mainframe."

Waters is quiet for a moment. "Did you get a peek at what cards our Security Directorate is holding?"

"Sort of." I hand him a wafer. "Whatever Trainor had, it's all here. You have my oath as a telepath that this is the only copy."

He chuckles. "Your sacred oath as a telepath? Sounds intriguing."

"The secret handshake is a bitch."

"Then it would seem that Mr. Trainor's future is in my hands."

"If you trust me, yes."

We are walking slowly. "Then I'd like to ask another favor."

"Oh? Which is?"

"I'd like you to kill Erasmus Trainor."

That stops me dead in my tracks. Everything I've done so far has been sanctioned by LAPD. Didi will spend the next week filling out paperwork on the shootings that I've participated in. Derrick and his superiors will have to sign off on each and every time I discharged my gun.

I doubt very seriously they will look the other way on a murder for hire. Worse, they would probably recast all of the other incidents to make me look like some vigilante gun nut.

"You realize that you have just committed a crime."

Richard holds the wafer in his hand so that it catches the light. "If you scanned any of this, you realize that it won't be the first time."

I have indeed scanned the file. Influence peddling for the most part, greasing the wheels of the globe to make commerce possible and profitable. No smoking gun there for anything that Erasmus Trainor may have done, although Trainor wouldn't keep a file on himself.

"That may be true. But I want no part of taking him down."

"Name your price."

"I have no price."

"You know the old saying. Everyone can be bought."

"I can't."

"Think about it. I'm sure that you can."

"Not for this. Not now. Not ever."

"Then how about dinner? At my place."

I look at Richard, his face partially hidden in shadow.

"Do we have more business to discuss?"

"No-o. What we have is old business to celebrate."

I nod absently. What we have is mystery piled on top of mystery. Didi has compared Riva's record autopsy to all of the phone numbers in my circle of suspects. There are sixty-three hits on Phillip VanMeer's private cell phone in the last three months. Sixty-three. That's a lot of golf, Phillip.

There were other things on the mainframe, too. Large transfers of credits into numbered accounts hidden away from the finance database where they should have been. Transfers that go back three years, the length of time that Waters Industries keeps records on-line. Derrick is siccing the fraud boys on those because we're talking big money. Big money. And then there's the kicker, the thing hidden among the Trainor files that isn't on the chip I've given to Richard, a file that I don't have the guts to scan just yet.

It's labeled, simply, JENNY.

Dinner. Fresh from near physical rape and absolutely consummated mind rape, and the man wants to crank open some bubbly and celebrate. Perhaps Richard is so studly that he thinks he can fuck me into pulling the trigger on Trainor.

Maybe not. Man has to have some brains. He's rich, isn't he?

Well, Daddy's rich. Maybe brains aren't his strong point.

And what do I expect to get from this meeting besides a meal? I'm not really sure. Certainly, more work from Waters Industries when this ghastly bit of sleuthing is over. Maybe someone in high financial places who owes me.

Maybe a clue or two. Maybe I expect Richard to make a pass at me, and maybe if there's enough Sytogene left in my head I'll let him do it.

A sleek black chopper rattles overhead at high speed. An executive make, I think, from the heavy sound of the rotors.

Richard's building is just ahead.

He's back in the mogul style of dress. Once again I am struck by how handsome he is, in a wealthy sort of way. The apartment is spacious, classically appointed, and sumptuously carpeted.

Dinner for two is set on the terrace complete with candlelight. The required champagne is in a gold-plated bucket.

He holds the chair out for me. A butler wheels in a serving cart and is dismissed.

There is a data card on my plate. It is clear, coated plastic with anodized aluminum at the edges.

"Nice place, Richard. Can't say I understand the choice of appetizers." I sit down.

"It's an incentive. For what we talked about today."

I finger the card. "How big an incentive?"

"Three million. Tax free. Money that has spent most of its life sunning in the Cayman Islands via the Seychelles."

"And completely untraceable."

He shrugs. "A philosopher once said 'you have to get rich in the dark.' "

"Does the money come with an investment plan?"

"Does the job convey any fringe benefits?"

"For the employer or the employee?"

"Employer."

My turn to shrug. "I doubt it."

He smiles. It is a killer smile, a killer's smile, something his face was always capable of but never before revealed.

I have Trainor's JENNY file loaded in the computer in my head. Three million to waste the source of this info suggests rather strongly that I take a peek. I think of the file folder and a software agent paging through it and the rest begins automatically.

"Does your father approve of your arrangements?" The smile vanishes as quickly as it dawned, and he looks out onto the hothouse that is LA almost every evening. He does not answer as the crackle of a distant thunderbolt ripples through the heavy air.

"I'll take that as a no."

"My father creates messes. I clean them up."

Richard pauses to serve dinner. Cuisine that looks pretty on the plates.

<accessing folder JENNY. two files embedded titled "telepath.model" and "sixa.medical.">

"And he created the Trainor mess."

"Let's say I need to protect him on this one."

<"telepath.model" contains 26-page report by doctor robert nicholson entitled "a predictive model for onset of spontaneous spongiform encephalopathy in telepaths" dated september, 2049.>

"For three million credits."

A nibble in the ensuing silence, a sip of the wine of kings. "I sense frustration, Richard."

"You have a gift for understatement, Jenny."

<scanning file "sixa.medical.">

I finger the data card and wait for the voice in my head and the voice in front of me to continue.

"A gift for understatement. Arnold built the business. I keep it going. I scope out new territories, new ideas, and Arnold makes the phone calls. Things happen. That's all business is, Jenny. Making things happen."

"Did you know a Genevive Wilkerson?"

The reaction, if it is there at all, is so slight, so imperceptible, that later I will replay the image in my head many times just to see if I'm kidding myself.

"No. At least I don't think so."

<"sixa.medical" file is dated today for transfax to jenny six alpha tomorrow.>

"Marie Folcoup?"

He shakes his head. "No."

"They were women who, at least on paper, could travel in your circle."

<this is a priority communications interruption from LAPD>

"Which means?"

"They were beautiful debutantes. And they're very dead."

"I'm not sure I understand this line of questioning. Surely I'm not a suspect?"

"There are no suspects. There are circles of overlap. There are victims, there are crimes, and there are questions."

He dabs his mouth with a napkin. "I suppose you're just doing your job."

<boss.>

"I suppose." *<not now, deeds!>*

"Then what about my job?"

<jen, this is derrick.>

"Not within the scope of my current abilities, I'm afraid." *<fuck off, trent.>*

Richard takes another slender data card out of his jacket.

"Then I'll up the price."

<jenny. we need you right now. get out of there.>

"How much? Just out of curiosity." *<not now, derrick!>*

"Six. Plus an investment plan. You'll double your money in a year."

"Desperate, eh, Richard?"

"And what of revenge, Jenny? What of your friend?"

"I . . ."

<there's another body, jenny. less than an hour old. we need you.>

Shit.

<cause of death?>

<spontaneous trauma. no other signs.>

"Revenge, Jenny? I'm willing to pay for what you want. To make amends."

"Not . . . my style, I'm afraid."

<who?>

<jacqueline vanmeer. phillip v's wife.>

"A pity."

There is a pad on the roof. We both turn at the sound of an approaching machine, the rotors getting louder and louder. There is a snick in my head as Derrick's intrusion ends.

<synopsis of file "sixa.medical" continues: *subject is a former piggybacker . . . predictive models suggest onset of encephalopathy in as little as six weeks . . . following symptomology as prp concentrates reach threshold . . .>*

* * *

It's a hell of a way to end a six-million-credit business meeting. For once I am unarmed, my weapon sitting in the glove of my p-car somewhere below. I left Richard wordless, but he didn't seem surprised. Another damn body in spooky circumstances. Another trip down memory lane.

"She was found in the walk-through refrigerator in the kitchen. Maid, I think. Looking for vegetables or some such." Derrick looks grimly out the window at the city sliding by below.

"The maid make the call?"

"No. VanMeer called himself. According to the black and whites that arrived on the scene first, VanMeer took off as they rolled up."

"Then he's implicated."

"Maybe. Do you think there's a connection?"

My head is still filled with soft cotton from the last remnants of Sytogene in my system. I'm not sure that I can do this. I'm not sure I want to do this.

"Maybe," I say cautiously. A fragment of suspicious thought from Derrick's mind floats through and then vanishes.

The skids thump down on the roof of an apartment building. Derrick tells me that it's one of those very exclusive high-rises with apartments scooped out of whole floors, or multiples thereof. We are hustled down the stairs into the penthouse apartment of Phillip and Jacqueline VanMeer.

"Which way?" A uniform points, and we rush into the kitchen.

Scandinavian style, perhaps a thousand square feet and enough equipment to make most restaurants envious. The woman on the floor is nondescript, an executive's wife acquired long ago for love or money or some other reason that may have been superfluous for years.

"Better hurry, Jenny. We're pushing the envelope on this one."

Hurry. Rush into hell. Run into the flames. Run, you freak. Run as fast as you can.

There is no time for procedure. If Didi is with me, she is silent as I kneel down, touching cold flesh. And I am frightened.

The light is blinding, the killer has overpowered her with his mind, driving her backward into the kitchen, a knife of pain that seems to saw away at her mind, all view of the killer, all perspective, obliterated.

The killer stands over her, his face and features blank, as if selectively erased. Her life ebbs quickly under his onslaught. And near the end, the killer's voice, also subtly altered, mutters the last words an uncomprehending victim will ever hear . . .

Remember Heaven?

I shrink back in horror because the thoughts are amplified, triggering a cascade of buried memories—

Demarche:

Cunt! Kill her!

Derrick:

protect her

and Him:

I know all about the past.

I love you anyway.

The voice is the same.
The killer is from Heaven.

BOOK TWO

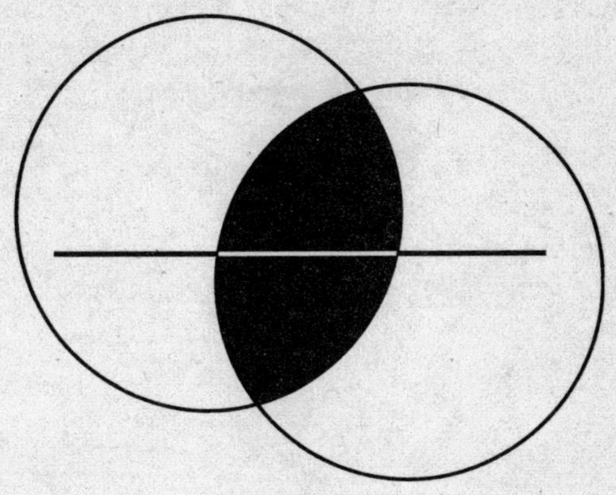

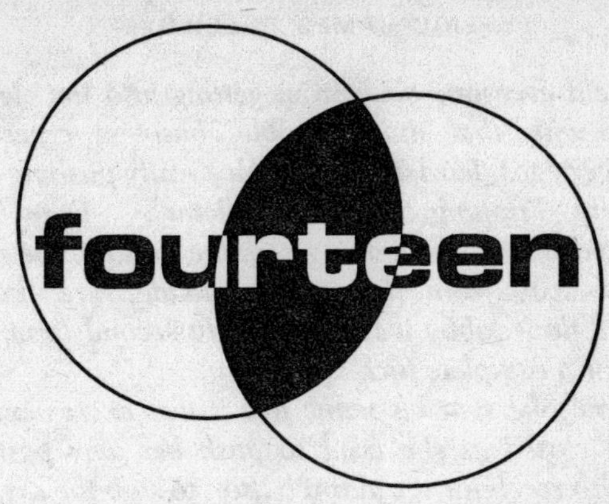

He could do her standing up. Her legs were that long.

you fucking incompetent. you idiot.

He had more than a sense by then that things were not right in his head. Checked out the research on his own. Avoided doctors, because then they'd know. He was desperate for Genevive and what she could tell him. Desperate. But she refused.

He pushed her, pushed her hard. Pursued her. Wined her. Dined her. Got rejected.

how in the world do you function? look at this mess you've made! look at it!

I SAID (pushing his head down) LOOK AT IT.

Tracked her moves. Decided that she would give him what he wanted. Picked a date, a time. A place.

* * *

Held everyone back from getting into the elevator. Hard with that many people, business types with stronger egos, harder to push. Not really pushing some, actually. Tripping them . . . brilliant . . . Even harder over a distance—he didn't get on the car until the second floor, away from the crowds. Made sure that the second-floor lobby was empty, split second timing, not bad for a complete fuck up . . .

You. She spat his name like it was excrement. The doors closed as she tried to push her way past him. Tried to reach for the alarm button to stop the car, communicate with the computer monitoring the lobby and the building's other vital functions. He pushed her back, she slapped him and he almost lost control—almost—as he turned the override key that made it a nonstop ride to the top of the building.

you don't deserve what i've given you

His fury smashed into her brain and her mind exploded under his onslaught like overripe fruit. Her eyes rolled up in her head, the whites showing as she slumped against the wall of the elevator, shaking. She was pathetic, wilted.

No *matter. He had what he wanted.*

He didn't fuck Genevive Wilkerson.

She didn't deserve it.

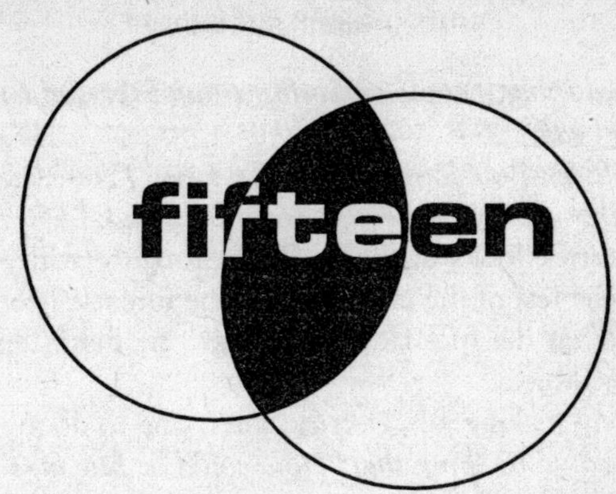

"Jenny?" The voice from a long distance in the middle of mental vertigo.

The start of it all, the start of my queer destiny as a freak.

"Jenny?" Louder now, hands shaking me.

I never could explain the voices in my head that night in Heaven. I never could explain why I suddenly jumped the scale to become what I am—a bit of personal fiction suggesting that it just fucking happened doesn't hold water anymore. *And the bad thing. . .*

"What happened? Did you see the perp?" Derrick Trent is holding me, dammit, like I'm some sort of invalid.

Did you see the perpetrator. Oh, yeah, I saw a perpetrator. I felt resonance cold and clear in my head like nothing I've ever felt before, like he has something of mine that I want back. *But how to explain this to Derrick?*

"I couldn't get a good look." *Officer Bob holds me in his arms, crying with me, the bad thing lying on the beach under a sheet, a blanket, people gathered around the bad thing, people gathering around the sudden pain in my head.*

Officer Bob looks me in the eyes. "You didn't do something, did you, Jenny? Something bad?"

Derrick looks at me, pulls me roughly aside, away from the rest of the uniforms and the forensic people.

"What the fuck are you doing?" he hisses through clenched teeth.

"My fucking job, Derrick. I'm trying to do my job." *How could he think that? How could he hug me when I shake my head no?*

"Not good enough. Something happened. You saw *something*. What was it?"

I shake my head. It's too amazing, too confusing.

"Don't meltdown on me, Jenny!"

I don't know whether to love or hate this mystery man, this Mr. Right. If he was somehow responsible for my becoming a full-fledged telepath than I have much to hate him for. Maybe I always had the ability and just repressed it. Maybe I needed to be slapped into awareness. Maybe I didn't want to wake up to this world, this ugly world of cruelty, this telescope into the heart of darkness.

<holding out on me. . . fuck is this?>

<call the captain. gotta pull her off the case . . .>

"Derrick, get me out of here, please."

<oh, yeah, jen, you're out of here all right.>

Even as we sit drinking coffee and discussing the facts of the latest murder I can hear the nonstop treachery in Derrick's mind, the inner rage masked by his dispassionate professional discourse. I feel sick, confused, terrified.

"Derrick, what if the killer is after something totally unexpected?"

"Like what?" He is reluctant to be pulled from his "dump the stupid piggybacker" reverie.

"Like me."

<huh?>

"Marie Folcoup. Genevive Wilkerson. Riva Barnes. And now Jacqueline VanMeer. They all had something in common that I've never told you about."

<marie . . . wilkerson . . .> Derrick is fixing the case files in his mind, getting the LAPD computer to dump the data burst directly into his head.

"Something in common?" He rubs his temple as the files come through.

"Marie Folcoup had an image of my name, JENNY, implanted in her mind by her killer. Genevive Wilkerson had the image JEN with a heart in her thoughts. It appeared as a tattoo on the leg of her killer.

"Riva Barnes had the image of my full name and alpha designation being woven into the carpet where she lay." *Rub my temples. Pounding in my head . . .*

"You mean this is a serial murderer. And a telepath. With the hots for you." *<can't say I blame him . . .>*

"More than that. This is someone from my past. That was the clue he left in Jacqueline VanMeer's head as she was dying."

"How distant? A former lover?"

"Very distant. Back at the beginning when I first discovered my talent. Back in Heaven."

He was there, too. "Just a voice in your head." *But I never figured out who the voice was, where it was coming from. Confusion—makes me dizzy to think about it . . .*

"Not any voice, Derrick. The first voice I ever heard without piggybacker equipment. The first."

"Not just overhearing his thoughts?"

"No. It was directed at me. He told me I was pretty." *He told me he knew about the bad thing from my past.*

Derrick is reeling. "How do you know it was him? I mean this particular guy."

I turn away, pretending to survey the crowd at the diner. Should I tell him how I know? Would he understand?

The fragment of thought in Jacqueline VanMeer's head lolling there in her elegantly appointed home. It was a fragment of memory tinged with the sounds of Heaven so long ago. The sunken living room. Demarche.

The music of that song—the feeling. Delicious, intoxicating.

I haven't felt it in ten years.

I haven't felt that way since that night.

That's how I know.

"You don't look so good."

"Yeah. I feel like shit."

Derrick Trent reaches into his pocket. "Here. Take one of these."

I stare at the little pill. "I'm on medication. I can't just take a trank."

"It's Sytogene, Jenny. Go on."

Sytogene . . . "You're a regular drugstore, Derrick."

"Um-hmm. Look, why didn't you tell me?"

The look on his face is all wrong. Derrick Trent has transcended being a police officer. All of the old feelings, the want, the caring, the lust, are all right there toying with the expression on his face, rippling through his mind . . .

"I didn't believe it at first. I . . . I wanted to find the killer. Riva's killer. Marie's killer. Genevive's. I thought it was a taunt. I didn't think I had anything to do with this, Derrick."

The old bad things have taken over his head. The old bad things that I have associated with men since I can remember, the earliest memories of the very notion of the opposite sexes.

"Don't touch me, Derrick."

"Jen, I didn't mean anything . . ."

"Don't."

don't.

don't.

"Jenny, you break my heart, you know that? You've gotten yourself into a place that no one can touch. It hurts me to see you wrapped up like this . . ."

"I won't sleep with you, Derrick. Just cut it out. Stop it."

We leave it like that, or I left it like that, because I walked out, suddenly preferring the harsh mental embrace of strangers.

It's a little after one in the morning when I get back to the office. I'm tired and my head is hurting from the activity of the last few hours. Didi wants to say something but my look shuts her up as I go into my inner sanctum.

The transfax machine sits in a corner of my private office. As I sit the desk chimes, indicating a file has been received. The desk blotter cursor is on an icon labeled:

Sixa.Medical

transfax hard copy to follow

And obediently the transfax machine beeps and a sheet of paper starts curling out. The first sheet reads:

Jenny Six Alpha
Medical Report
Submitted by: Robert Nicholson, MD

Maybe the whole damn thing is a hoax. "Deeds!"

She's at the door instantly. "Yeahboss."

"I just got a datafile and a transfax. Track down the source, please?"

She walks over to the transfax machine, glances at the settings. Touches a few buttons. Waits a couple of seconds.

The machine chirps.

"The transfax is from UCLA Medical Center. Robert Nicholson, MD. Want me to check the source of the datafile?"

The second page curls out of the machine. Then a third. Then the transmittal report. Didi stands there silent all the while waiting for me to say something.

"Uh, no. No thanks."

I gather the other two pages and set them in the middle of my desk. And stare at them silently.

The transfax machine beeps again. A page begins curling out. The heading looks the same. Maybe Didi's answerback confirmation was mistaken for a retrans request.

The first sheet drops into the tray. Then the transmittal report. Just the cover page? I walk over to the machine. Odd, the transmittal report is blank. I scoop the first page of the medical report and the transmittal out of the tray. Glance at the first page of the medical report.

Ohmigod. I drop the pages and scream.

Didi comes running, stares at the page lying on the floor. It says:

Jenny Six Alpha
Medical Report
Submitted by: Robert Nicholson, MD

And in crude lettering underneath the title:

DO YOU WANT TO LIVE FOREVER?

Didi checks. She can't trace the transfax.

The phone rings. Didi and I both stare at it, the light blinking on my receiver. Line one.

My head is starting to throb again. I pick up the receiver.

It's a vidphone transmission, breaking up with static like there's a huge electrical flux in the background. The figure in the picture has his back turned, like he's purposefully blocking the camera with his back. It could be VanMeer. It could be anyone.

The voice is a whisper. *"Miss Sixa."*

"Yes."

He gives me an address. *"Meet me there in one hour."*

"Why?"

Nothing at first.

"Meet me if you want answers." And he begins to turn toward the camera pickup.

And the picture fades to a dot.

sixteen

He had minutes, if that. This was the last strategic target that he had. One last push, then he could give up this sorry business.

Security was a problem. He studied it for months on end, preparing for it, considering the possibilities, rejecting them all because they compromised him in one way or another.

Here were the problems:

1) The roof was too secure. Pressure sensitive alarms, no easy access to it, even from an adjoining property. It would take a bomb to get into the heating and ventilation shed on the roof and into the building. Too many things that could be traced.

2) The lobby was also too secure. Cameras, external monitors. Human doormen with AI's as back-up, police response within minutes, given the address. He might as well send a postcard if he walked out that way.

* * *

Magic. It would require more than a little magic. He found a woman in the building whom he could stand to sleep with occasionally. Assumed a different identity just for her, flashed some cash, pushed her mind a bit. Arranged his schedule for an alibi, it would be close, for sure. On the appointed day went into the building wearing a hat pulled low, kept his face away from the camera, a good two hours before he planned to pull off the job.

Had routine sex. Left quickly. Made his way upstairs to the VanMeer apartment and hung in the shadows on the stairwell. Easy because the perimeter security was considered foolproof. No detection equipment in the stairwells, nothing! By now his sex partner would think that he'd left the building, would never think to connect him to the crime.

He knew Mrs. VanMeer's husband wasn't home. Reached past the door and found the maid's mind, forced her to remember an errand that required her to leave the apartment, made her leave the front door open. Entered and surprised Jacqueline VanMeer, shoved her toward the kitchen. Whistling while he worked. Pressing her down to the floor of the walk-in refrigerator, singing softly to her as he bulldozed her brain, singing something Jenny would remember, getting that old feeling from so long ago—

. . . turning the killing impulse just so, so she would get the flavor of it when she touched Jacqueline VanMeer's flesh, the same yearning he'd tried to put there in the beginning. The circle was complete.

Oh, yes. The message. Whispered into Jacqueline VanMeer's ear, with love to Jenny.

He compromised himself getting out, though. Hopefully, it wouldn't matter.

The mystery message brings me to an old grey lady of a warehouse built at a time when assassins prowled the routes of presidential motorcades with high-powered rifles and people still had innocence that could be touched by the notion of national tragedy. Concomitant with its age is its aura of disrepair and disuse. The fence is down in places and the only signage that I see is crusted over and barely readable—

DELTEC INDUSTRIES

The name should've been my first clue that something was wrong. It wasn't.

I leave the p-car on the street, locked up snug against the desolation. My heels click against the pavement as I thread my way into the place. Every step is an effort that shoots pain into my temples. I thought of Sytogene before I left the office and deferred. Nicholson's vial is back at the apartment, anyway. *Of course, I could have taken Derrick's . . .*

Once past the decrepit exterior I find that this is indeed a functioning facility, perhaps the facade is just for show. I wonder why Mr. Right wants to meet me here. "Meet me if you want answers," he said, rather cryptically.

The interior is lit by emergency lights, even though expensive sodium vapor lamps hang overhead. Okay, I'm here, where are you? I relax and let my senses probe the vast interior for sentience. It feels odd to have to extend my abilities like this; usually I am trying my best to curtain the oppressive noise.

<you're mine now, sweetheart.>

The engine, a very late model internal combustion job, fires and seems oppressively loud and smelly even in the far reaches of the central chamber of the building. Headlamps to my right snap on as tires squeal. The car, dark blue or black, comes barreling out of hiding, smashing a series of crates as it accelerates. Toward me.

Now this doesn't present much of a moral dilemma. Try and run me down and I'll fuck you up. The speed of the thing is amazing—the little electrics just don't have the kind of torque to get that much steel moving in that much of a hurry in that short a distance.

Nerves of steel aside, this becomes a rather simple problem in marksmanship. My gun is out and ready, sight lines drawn as the target fades to a blur on the barrel sight. Squeeze, kick! Squeeze, kick! Squeeze, kick!

No effect. I just put a pattern with a spread of perhaps an inch or two that should have destroyed the driver's head. Even if he has a little pointy one.

At the last possible moment I step aside and let the behemoth roar past. The sound doesn't help my head any. It skids and slews around on two tires for a sec until all the rubber catches and leaves scorched tracks on the smooth concrete. I use this delta v maneuver to pump more shells into the vehicle—they spark against an armored hide but do not penetrate.

Bulletproof glass, too. You better . . .

The car cranks up again, juking side to side. . . . Run! Run goddammit!

. . . I swear I set some sort of high jump record as the car careens toward me . . . half a jump and a scramble up the side of a big packing crate filled with something heavy like machinery because it doesn't tip under my weight, the bumper kisses the wood and splinters it, turning the mother like a merry-go-round. My grip on the pistola and the box are very tenuous indeed.

The driver fishtails into a dead stop with tires smoking, blasts into reverse, right at me . . .

. . . go for the tires . . . two-handed grip, c'mon, Jenny, take the tires out, you are a *markswoman* . . .

impact! that sends me flying as the box flies backward with kinetic transference.

there I go, there I go, there I go, *limp, stay limp, resist the urge to stick out a hand and break the fall* . . .

I catch the floor more or less on my side and skid across it on my back. Gun's still in my hand. Have to sit up, oh, *shit*! I hear that ugly growl and grind as the gears engage, I'm out here in the *open*! Here it comes, here it comes, my shots spanking the metal and the rubber until the hammer falls on an empty chamber, legs won't work, can't get up—

I throw my hands in front of my face as the car skids

into me, the driver leaning on the brakes and cranking the wheel to the right . . .

Perhaps it is my left wrist breaking that I hear as the door slaps against my arms and slams me across the floor. Perhaps that is wishful thinking as the lights go out.

My left arm is numb. I wish my back were. Body parts that I'd prefer were no longer attached hurt like hell. I open my eyes sprawled some twenty feet from where the black automobile sits, my gun five feet from my outstretched right hand. Gun. As in have to reload . . .

"Not so fast, honey."

Erasmus Trainor is pulling off a pair of black leather driving gloves as he strolls into my field of vision. He places a black-booted foot squarely on my left wrist and lovingly applies a tiny bit of pressure.

See ya! The pain is so intense that I black out . . .

. . . and back into reality with a jolt.

"Guess it hurts, huh?" He chuckles and lights a cigarette. "Didn't want to kill you without having some quality time, Ms. Sixa." He chuckles again. "Quality time. Hah!"

"You killed Eddie Reynolds, didn't you?"

"Who? You mean the nigger at the warehouse? Nope." He waggles a finger at me. "And I didn't kill the girly girl you found in there, either."

"Who did?" I manage to gasp.

"Don't know."

"Susan Bentsen?"

Trainor smiles. "Orders."

"Jeremy Bentsen?"

"Too stupid to let live."

"Jacqueline VanMeer?"

"Don't know the lady." He grinds the cigarette out about a millimeter from my damaged wrist and I cringe. "Q & A is over, bitch."

"Wait! Why . . . did you have my file? My medical file?"

<what file.?> "What file?" He looks at me quizzically. Then raises his voice. "Should I kill her, boss?"

Another set of footsteps. My visual field is limited and the figure comes from a darkened part of the warehouse. I can't touch his mind. Could this be Mr. Right?

"No." The new figure stoops over and picks up my gun with gloved fingers. He looks at me and then extracts a fresh clip from my bag.

"I think I should do the honors for a change," Richard Waters says quietly.

Waters looks me in the eye and thinks—

Jenny

as he ejects the spent clip and inserts the fresh one.

"Nice work," he says to Trainor as he sort of fiddles with the gun. He seems unsure how to use it.

"Jesus Christ, stop fucking around! You trying to get me killed?" Trainor steps toward Richard to take the pistol from his hands.

"Killed? You? You might say that."

The gun barks twice and Trainor falls to the ground, hit once in the chest and once in the head.

* * *

Richard bends down and presses the gun into my hand.

"Why?" I manage to croak. My head feels like a ripe melon Trainor worked over with a lead pipe.

He places a gloved finger to his lips, kisses it, and places it against my mouth.

"Remember my offer. Don't mention that I was here and the money is yours, Jenny."

"But . . ."

"Shssh. A 'passerby' has already called the police." He pulls a capsule from his jacket and breaks it under my nose. "Rest now. And remember the words 'self-defense' are worth three million credits apiece."

He turns and begins walking away, but by the time he straightens up I'm in la-la land.

eighteen

Derrick comes to visit me in the hospital. While he doesn't exactly pronounce Riva's case closed, he does say that Trainor's death ties up a lot of loose ends for the department.

"But Trainor wasn't a telepath," I say. My left arm is done up in a fingertip to elbow cast.

"We think Freddie Barnes is the missing link. He killed that girl that was there, a-hem, with you, for example."

"And the other two cases? Genevive Wilkerson? Marie Folcoup?"

"Possibly unrelated. You said yourself that there was no obvious link between the victims."

"Except for Mr. Right. Except for the clues the killer left me."

Derrick shrugs. When LAPD shrugs, it means they're satisfied even if I'm not.

"Waters Industries has paid off pending capture of Freddie Barnes."

"Pending?"

"C'mon, Jen, you know how these things work. Money moves from one escrow account to another. It's all pseudo-legal bullshit." *Why is he so anxious to close the case?*

"Yeah, I bet." Arnold Waters sent me a nice "Get Well" card. I'd say the gesture is about six mil short of touching my heart.

Especially since I've kept my end of the bargain.

"So have you thought any more about my little proposition?" Derrick is looking out the window at the grey haze.

"Move in with you for a while?" I can't bring myself to say "until the end."

"I've got four weeks coming to me," he says defensively. He's been talking to Nicholson. Never-never time is approaching.

"And all you want to do is take care of me?"

Hands raised in contrition. "Honest. Separate rooms, the whole nine."

"I'll think about it."

I must admit, all of my misgivings about men and normals aside, Derrick isn't a bad guy. He'd stay on his toes for me. God knows he's been persistent enough. God knows I'm in no position to be picky.

There's just one problem. A curiosity fueled by a kiss the last time I saw him.

I wonder why Richard hasn't called me.

It's discharge day. Three weeks of crummy hospital food, bitchy nurses, and horny doctors could cure death as far as I'm concerned. Let me outta here!

Derrick comes with a bouquet of flowers intending to escort me home. Didi comes with a list of things I have to do to rehab my wrist, as well as some urgent messages from neglected clientele. Ah, Deeds. Where would I be without you to maintain my fiction of long life?

"You'd probably be poorer, but happier, boss."

Derrick and Didi escort me down to the ground floor. Didi arranges for my bill to be transfaxed to Waters Industries (hey, it isn't six mil but four hundred pages of printout can't be peanuts). I refuse a wheelchair, mainly because both Derrick and Didi are fighting over who gets to push.

"Ms. Sixa?"

I turn. Some man in a suit I don't recognize. "Would you come this way, please?"

My blood coagulates. Is this guy from the DA's office, come to ask me more questions? Has Richard 'fessed up?

He leads me to another waiting room, just another way out of the hospital, Didi and Derrick in tow. The waiting room is filled not with people, but with flowers. Filled. The scent is something you'd expect at the Botanical Gardens. Christ, it's gorgeous; instantly I smell a rat.

"I'm not sure I under . . ."

"Mr. Waters sends his regards. Through that far door, if you please?" Ah, yes. The rich rat wants more than the hole in his pocket.

The far door leads to another world. Outside, facing the pavement in the smoky sun, my two escorts a step behind me.

Richard Waters stands in front of the open door of a mag-lev limousine with a single bloodred rose in his hand. He takes my hand warmly, kisses me on the cheek, his mind as strong as the sheer cliff of a mountain behind my 30ccs of Sytogene.

"A deal's a deal," he says softly. "I've been in Egypt."

"And I want my money," I say, smiling. And won't he be surprised at what *isn't* included in the deal. The interior of the limousine is so cold I need a sweater. Didi and Detective Trent are left behind, openmouthed.

"This isn't about sex, Jenny. It's about power. It's about the flip side to the rest of the stinking world. It's about capabilities that only money can provide. Let me show you."

The next three weeks are a whirlwind. I have now become intimately familiar with the Transportation Lifestyles of the Rich and Famous. I can tell which of the executive jets we're in by the details of the upholstery, by the subtle accents of the flight crews. Vera is my favorite, head stew of the big Gulfstream that does transoceanic duty for Waters Industries.

Richard has been kind and caring. His touch, although suggestive, hasn't strayed beyond the boundaries of propriety, although I am now beginning to wonder about more than the suggestive hand on my shoulder at Ipanema beach. He's quite a hardbody under the execusuits, and cuts a mean figure in a pair of skimpy Speedos. It's funny how things work. If he'd wanted me I would have run.

I would have run far. But the sense I get from him—is he lonely in some way? In, perhaps, most ways? Isolation I can understand because the real world like Rio is depressing, surrounded as we are by Richard's private army of security. The gold watch on Richard's wrist could feed fifty people for a month in this town based upon my glimpses of the poverty that butts up against the security phalanx. But Richard strikes me as not just lonely, but alone.

Moscow is chilly and clear. This was a brief stop as Richard hobnobbed with the president of the republic. He says something about offering to buy the Ukraine back for Russian solidarity and lower food prices, and everyone in the entourage, including me, laughs. Paris I've visited before, although Richard spends a tremendous amount of time with me, arm in arm, sightseeing.

Oh, yes. The money. I have a clear wafer couriered back to my office in LA from LAX on the way out. At our first stop is a message from Didi that is just a number with a credit sign in front of it, and little smiley faces in all those zeros. In a way I'm more like Richard now that I've added wealthy to my list of lonely and afraid. In a sense Richard's right; the world isn't about sex after all. It's about the damage necessitated by the lack of love, implied by the exercise of power by loveless men, loveless women, circling the globe in private jets.

Too bad the money won't buy me time. Richard has learned to ignore the lapses in my concentration, or when my step falters as we thread through a receiving line. At least I haven't developed a twitch yet. According to Nicholson that's the last gasp of my healthy brain before the onslaught begins. In sheep, scrapie produces brain matter that's pitted and degenerative. How long do I really have to live? A long time. How long before I begin dying? A short time.

Richard is an astute businessman who shares the details of the intercontinental sprawl of his enterprise as we flit from paradise to banquet. He is a master negotiator, able to pick up the subtlest nuance in his adversaries as easily as I might have picked up their thoughts. I have been on a crash course with Waters Industries the topic. Nights I lay in a sumptuous bed and think about Richard in another suite of rooms down the hall or on another floor, both of us more alone because of the opulence.

During such nights my fears of my fatal disease rise up like heat on a summer day, lighter than air, more oppressive. Dying and dying alone, the futility of it all, the truth of what I've been missing wells up in me like a balloon ready to burst. There's something incredibly fatalistic about running away from who we are, from others. There's something incredibly flawed in *visions* of running away in a jet airplane, or to a drug, or into a feeling of inadequacy. Our naivete of escape denies that wherever we go, there we are. Our arrogance of wanting ignores that no matter what we have *joy is fleeting*.

<and no amount of personal perfection can maintain the high.>

When I touch his perfect fucking shoulder under his perfect fucking suit at some gala reception for some mega deal, I hope my fingertips convey to Richard how sorry I feel for him. In return, I fully expect Richard to feel sorry for me; I expect him to be as *capable* of pity as I am *capable* of reading someone's thoughts.

All good things come to an end. We are in a holding pattern above LAX, the big Gulfstream too heavy for the private runway that Richard uses for smaller craft. There is a stage five pollution alert, fueled by temperature inversions and a wildfire burning out of control in South Centro.

As we circle we can see the black palls of smoke rising over massive fires and national guard troops deployed around the perimeter of the dead zone. The news says that they have shoot to kill orders for anyone trying to bust the zone, and I think, guiltily, about Zack Millhouse and Eddie Reynolds caught below in the firestorm. This is as depressing an end to a glorious run as I can imagine, and we cover the same turf over and over again, each time the plane banks and I find myself staring at scarred and tortured earth.

Richard joins me in the aisle seat, puts his arm around me, and I don't object. He signals Vera for champagne, as if the scene below and the end of our trip are something to celebrate. She hands him two glasses, one for me, and a thin black velour case.

"Your thoughts?" he asks, a hidden smile waiting at the corners of his mouth.

"I'd prefer Paris," I say, angling my head at the window to the destruction below.

He hugs me closer, the closeness welcome even if it is, perhaps, our last run.

"I'd prefer you," he says softly. He looks into my eyes.

"You have a proposition?"

"I think you should know what you're getting into."

"I have a pretty good idea."

"Do you?" He pulls away. Opens the velour case. *A neural interface . . .*

The contents send me sliding down a sheer cliff of fear, of memory. I turn away, South Centro somehow more comforting than what Richard Waters is asking of me.

"Everything has a price, Jenny." His lips move to brush my cheek and I turn away. "Even intimacy."

Vera comes by. "We just got clearance. We'll be on the ground in fifteen minutes."

After Heaven comes hell. After my brief stint in the normals sex industry, after Mr. Right reached in and opened my head . . .

. . . the flat black instrument, oscillator dials and simple slide controls, a headset for input . . .

. . . Eduardo and Matilda, the old crone and her boy toy who wanted to use my body as a receptical for their lust . . . *i bought you, bitch, spread your legs* . . . the ultimate perversion of talent, the ultimate surrender. Hell was men who wanted me to play their game of Russian roulette. Heaven would have been a continuous nightmare of Matildas and Eduardos, young studs who can't get it up for wrinkled tired bodies regardless of the money, men who want to know what a girl feels when she touches herself, abuse, bondage. All the realm of experience, of kicks, are available in live out of body realism with a piggybacker whose price you can meet. I did this young and it made me old, I did this to assuage my shame at what I'd become. I did it until I couldn't stand it anymore, did it until that night in Heaven when I became a powerful telepath, one who didn't need to mess around with somebody else's cheap thrills. Ironic, isn't it, that in the end the fourth pull on the trigger happened without me knowing it.

Richard's device brings me back to all of it, all of the depravity, like rubbing your hand over an old scar and feeling the punishment that deformed your flesh. Yes,

Richard, even intimacy has its price, the ultimate price that I'd paid stupidly so long ago, something worse than sex in my opinion, more hideous, the true depths of Mr. Right's "gift" to me . . .

The gentle bump of Fernando's landing saves me from the abyss in my head. *From the bad thing that lurks . . .*

This time.

It's been a long flight. Vera is handing out re-breathers for LA's fouled air. Richard keeps his distance.

"Even intimacy has a price." It's more than a kiss. It's more than the key to all of this. It requires the past and the present to merge like the plates of the earth's crust, grinding together to produce a seismic event. How can he possibly ask this of me?

Later in the backseat of the mag-lev Richard reaches for me, the device no doubt tactfully packed away in the trunk. The warmth of his touch, the fleeting thoughts of affection that leak in through my chemical screen, thoughts that are killing me slowly.

"We just have to stop at the office for a moment, then we'll take you wherever you want to go, okay?" I nod, and Richard smiles as I look out the window. I haven't said precisely what I want as my destination, and Richard is too much the gentleman to ask.

The limo pulls into the parking lot. It is late, the lot is practically deserted, the long black slab of steel and glass is mostly dark. Richard steps out and walks briskly to the building. I get out of the car to think, leaving the driver, silent and well trained, to his own thoughts.

It is coincidence that I am looking at the building

when the light in the southwest corner snaps on. Richard is there, glances down into the lot, and waves. Weakly, I wave back, barely managing a smile that he can't possibly see from that height.

As he turns away the blast rips through the office, and Richard Waters vanishes in a deadly plume of glass and debris ejected outward so that flaming embers land at my feet. Three sets of opaque glass have been blown outward, the roar and the heat so fantastic that I sink to my knees.

The driver is out of the car on his wrist radio, frantically calling for help, as if all the ambulances in the world could work a miracle for Richard Waters.

There can't be anything left.

<lover boy is burning, melting away, fat slabs caressed by a blowtorch's hiss . . .>

What if you've mistaken loneliness for emptiness?

<the closest thing you've had to a lover boy; cooking flesh, liquified bones, carbon black . . .>

yeah, and telepathy just fills the hole, fills it the way a voyeur does . . .

<pathetic, jen. pathetic.>

fills it by listening, too afraid to act. too afraid to experience. too afraid of bad things . . .

When he watched her he felt in his heart that she was meant to be his and no one else's. He'd seen that clearly the first night in Heaven. She wasn't just anybody's girl, she was Jenny. His girl. It was nice to think about someone so special for a change, someone with whom he had a connection deeper than money or sex.

He'd saved her that night. Given her the edge she needed to make a life of her own, to prepare her to be a part of his life, to understand what it was like to have people's sick thoughts pouring into your head. He knew she'd understand, because he'd seen beyond the beauty to her core that first instant of contact with her mind. And nothing in the ensuing ten years had changed his opinion of her.

She even cares about the niggers, he marveled, as he plucked from her mind her gratitude for Zack Millhouse for saving her life. Niggers, for God's sake. Odd for someone as strong as she was to care about the zone or anybody in it.

Just another thing he was lacking. One of many. Her parents were normal, not like his. She still had warm thoughts for her father and mother, had thought about them that night in Heaven. Seduced by her beauty and her talent, not her upbringing. Not the first pretty girl to end up in the slush pile in Los Angeles, just as he was not the first to be a casualty of youth.

She complemented him. That's what he'd felt when he saw clearly what Demarche had in store for her. A little trauma is good for the soul, Jenny.

A little trauma. And then he'd pushed through. Connected with her pain, made her feel the intensity of pain as the gateway to power.

Power. The power to care. The power to kill. The power to buy and sell. The power to steal someone's heart. The power to change thoughts . . . the power to make him complete, to make up for the missing parts, the nasty grinding poverty of his psyche.

He loved her. He needed her.

He didn't know what he'd do without her.

He didn't know if he could survive rejection. Not from her. No Jenny. Hate me. Refuse me. But please don't reject me. Not until you know who I am. What I've done for you.

Please . . .

*   *   *

And in the back of his mind coiled like a snake the thought:

Don't reject me, Jenny. I'm not sure you'll survive if you do.

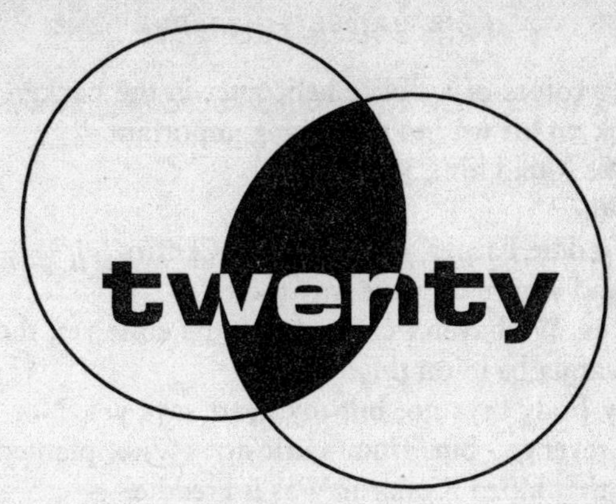

twenty

"Jenny, look, I'm sorry, but we have to do this." Derrick Trent and I are in the LA County Morgue. He nods to the bored-looking attendant, who opens the metal drawer and unwraps the specimen within.

"Too much destruction for a DNA match, Jen. We have to do this."

The attendant shows me the crumbling blackened flesh. It is the approximate size of a man's forearm, although the crumbled mass at the end could hardly be called a hand with fingers.

I nod to the attendant. The only body part of Richard Waters large enough to identify has been positively ID'd by the gold wristwatch cum communicator fused into the burnt flesh of his arm.

Didi keeps her distance. The tremblors in my hands are getting worse, the headaches a nonstop jackhammer at my temples. Gone with Richard is my chance at a cure, the final clue to the mystery of Celludyne. Gone . . . gone . . .

Derrick Trent calls me, audio only. I can hear the

beating rotors of a police helicopter in the background, Derrick on his way to something important.

"We found him, Jen."

"Who?"

"Freddie Barnes. He's in South Centro."

"And you're on your way there."

"Yes. We haven't crossed into the zone yet, though. You wanna be in on this?"

My body says no, but my heart says yes. Not quite from revenge, but from curiosity. Who planted the bomb that killed Richard? Was it Freddie?

"Yeah, Derrick. I want to be in on this."

"Okay." He pauses, shouts something to the pilot. "Ten minutes, Jen. Be on the roof. Okay?"

"Right."

And if it wasn't Freddie, maybe I want to make sure that he lives to tell.

The chopper sets down in the middle of a South Central conflagration, twin vortexes of smoke curling around the whirling blades. Half a block is burning, burning to the ground without the slightest bit of intervention from the authorities. The way it's always been. The way it always will be.

"How long have we got!" Derrick shouts at the pilot as he opens the door. The noise from the spinning turbine has not abated. The pilot looks out the canopy at the confining flames, the wind and the smoke from the fires. He shakes his head.

"Ten, maybe fifteen minutes at the outside. Dispatch says this area isn't secure. Gun battle a few blocks away. Headed in this direction."

"You wait for us, y'hear?" Derrick jabs his finger at the pilot.

"If the wind shifts we're all toast. No guarantees, Detective!"

"No! You wait!" Derrick propels himself through the door, myself in tow. He has his gun drawn.

The two LAPD birds have set down in the middle of the street. As we hit the pavement a building to our left collapses with a *whoomppb!* of heat and flames. The heat is fantastic.

Derrick runs crouched under spinning blades to the five-man SWAT team standing by. They are dressed in black, which must be fantastically uncomfortable in the heat. I follow, wanting to hear his instructions.

"What's your load?" Derrick shouts to somebody named Dominguez, who must be in charge of this band.

"Three guys," Dominguez shouts back, "are pushing low velocity darts filled with tranks and that Sytogene stuff. They're the sharpshooters. Me and Richardson"—he points to one of his men—"are pushing standard high velocity slugs. Stopping power just in case."

"Where is he?" I ask, and Derrick points straight ahead at a dilapidated building. Even on this, the right side of the street, only minutes remain before everything is consumed in fire.

"How much you wanna bet the sonofabitch is hiding on the roof?"Derrick asks.

It will take minutes to search the building. Minutes we don't have.

It's a three-story tenement. I'm thinking we need more men to do this, but Derrick's little posse will have to do. Derrick kicks in what's left of the front door, steps back in case of gunfire, counts to three.

We're in. Down low, combat style, the exertion is a problem for me, my own gun still in its holster because I don't think I can carry the weight and move at the same time. Dominguez and another SWAT guy head into the basement, calling out *"Police, come out with your hands up!"* as they descend the rickety stairs.

Derrick is ahead of me, checking room to room, gun at the ready. Nothing in the front parlor, nothing in the tiny bathroom. Rats scurrying in the tiny kitchenette, amazing that people have to live like this.

A SWAT guy splinters the back door, checks out the porch. Nothing.

"What'd I tell you. The fuck is up on the roof," Derrick says.

Derrick's radio squawks. No wireless in the zone. "Basement's clean."

"Right. How much time?"

"We been in here three minutes."

"Okay. We're going up the stairs to the second floor. Keep one man posted near the front in case we missed him and he tries to leave, over."

"Done."

Up the stairs, Derrick taking them two at a time. At the top, he stops, holds up his hand. Three bedrooms. A noise from one of them. I can hear moaning in my head.

First door kickdown. Nervous men with rifles swinging in arcs, covering the tiny space. Nothing.

Second door. Dominguez is coming up the stairs, I can hear his thoughts.

Nothing in the second bedroom.

Third door. Derrick kicks it open, and I see his gun come up—

<gotcha, Freddie.>

in his thoughts, but he doesn't shoot. When I get to the entrance I can see the woman lying bound on the bed. She's naked. Black, not unattractive, looks to be in her twenties. She's alive.

<shit.> "You, take her down, get her outta here." Derrick speaks to one of Dominguez's people like he was an errand boy.

This room stinks. Smells like Freddie was here alright. As she and I make eye contact a gout of flame out the window catches my eye. The building next to this one—

Explodes in a roar of flame and debris. The windows shatter, the concussion knocks me into Derrick.

"Trent, we gotta beat feet! The whole block's gonna go!" over Derrick's radio. The chopper pilot.

"No, goddammit! You stay put, you hear me! Stay put or I'll have your ass!"

A tongue of flame is licking the outside of this building.

Derrick helps me up. "You still up for this?"

I nod. "Okay. C'mon." He goes to the shattered window, lifts one leg, then the other over the sill onto the fire escape. The rusty metal groans under his weight. In front of him the building is burning with a bit more vigor.

"This way!" he shouts, the look in his eye something I won't forget. A cloud of black smoke blows in through the window, obscuring him for a second. Dominguez and I climb onto the fire escape trying to hold our breath against the dark clouds enveloping us.

"We don't have all day, people!" Derrick shouts. He's climbing the fire escape ladder to the roof.

The roof tar is bubbling from the heat; pieces of wood from the explosion next door litter the place lying in little pools of fire. The smoke is so bad I can't see the street. I can't see anything, except Derrick.

He's crouched down, shouting into his radio. Dominguez moves to our left to flank Derrick, check out the roof inch by inch. The other SWAT guy moves to the right.

"You're going to have to lift us off the roof!" A snatch of Derrick's radio call drifts back on the wind.

"Say again, you're breaking up!" the radio crackles back.

There is a creaking sag as the building shifts a little. I can see flames shooting up into the air behind us. Where the fire escape is.

Gunfire. Three shots from my right and behind.

"I saw him! I saw him!" The SWAT guy is pointing. All I see is smoke.

There. Ten yards away from me. Freddie Barnes, a little dart sticking out of his leg, cursing, ranting. He has a gun.

The brain sends the signal to my arm and hand, which don't respond quickly enough. Dominguez is too far to my left, obscured by the smoke; he's out of the play.

Two cracks of the pistol. The SWAT guy is down, two bullets having thumped him in the chest, heavy calibers from the look of agony on his face, in all likelihood two ugly bruises on his breastbone that he will thank the Kevlar people for.

Freddie and his pistol turn toward me.

"Police! Drop your weapon!" Derrick screams, and a piece of the roof sags again.

<i didn't kill anybody.>

Freddie thinks. He's looking at me as if I'm supposed to understand.

"Don't fucking move, asshole!" Derrick screams. The roof shifts again. My skin feels like it's about to catch fire.

"Don't shoot!" Freddie yells, but Derrick keeps the gun trained on him. Something deep in the bowels of the building goes up in an explosion and the place rocks real bad.

"Jenny! Tell him not to shoot me!" Freddie cries as a peal of thick smoke washes over him.

Derrick stands with his pistol in a two-handed grip, wiping his tearing eyes on his sleeve.

Freddie reappears, hands up, his eyes watering. "Just get me down," he whimpers. He begins to lay the gun on the roof.

"I said freeze, asshole!" Derrick screams, and his gun barks twice and Freddie Barnes is knocked down by the center mass impacts.

I run forward, wanting to connect with him, to find the cure, have to find the cure, but Derrick holds me back as Freddie's life bleeds away onto the soft black tar. Twin vortexes of smoke from a chopper's blades coming close, the wind and the corruption of the day blowing hard in my face, the roof precarious. Dominguez beside us suddenly, pulling his wounded man toward the hovering chopper.

"Joint's gonna blow, evac, evac!" Derrick's radio cackles, and I look into his eyes.

<i love you, jenny. i always have.>

but what's love got to do with it? I need to close the circle, to find a killer and the solution to the mystery. I need to find Celludyne and the link to all of this, and it looks like I never will.

The chopper hauls us off the roof, and my last sight is Freddie Barnes lying prone, his blood bubbling in a sea of melting black tar.

Didi has offered me the sanctity of the bin farm, but I have refused. Back at the office I ask her to leave, go home, and prop my one souvenir from this adventure, the black velour case, on the chair facing me. The case is solved according to Derrick and LAPD. Freddie's body proves that the case is over. But questions nag me.

Celludyne. Richard. Riva. What's the connection between a SWAT team in the ghetto looking to burn me down and Freddie Barnes?Why was Erasmus Trainor so ready to kill me? I'd said that I thought the reason had to be money, but Freddie Barnes had none.

And why, intriguingly enough, did Derrick Trent seem so anxious to close the case? Why did he have Sytogene that night when VanMeer's wife was discovered? What use could Sytogene be to him?

Then there's Richard. The official investigation has turned up no clues, even though LAPD will probably pin the bomb on poor Freddie Barnes. I can close my eyes and see it—

He waves, the explosion. Pieces of glass, furniture, lumps of circuitry merged with his body and blasted to the pavement in front of me, the violence of a split second of visuals more horrible than Ada Quinn's death by remote control.

More shocking than Richard's death is his apparent innocence. The neural interface would have given me access to all of Richard's thoughts, despite my revulsion. Perhaps his offer was a declaration of his innocence, and at least part of me wanted it to be. That's why I considered it, hoping that my instincts would be nullified by true intimacy.

Instead all I will ever have is possibilities forever unexplored. Long silences between us that felt more comfortable and comforting than anything I've ever known—

<almost lover boy burnt in the fire, emptiness, not just loneliness.>

Gone. All gone. And if Celludyne had some miracle, my access to that is gone now, too.

When the phone lights up, I pick it up without thinking. The telltale that signifies the vidphone is dark. Audio only. I think it's Didi.

Alas, my story has room for another surprise or two. The voice at the other end is distorted by electronics. It says precisely in clipped tones—

"Do you want to live forever?"

A last question. A final answer. An address not far from Didi's bin farm once again on the spooky side of legit LA.

Enough already. I pick up my weapon and turn out the lights to go.

Phillip VanMeer meets me at the entrance to what looks like a corrugated steel prefab. He is wearing coveralls that are darkly stained. He motions me inside without a word.

The inside is empty, or at least relatively. No souped-up deathmobiles from a forgotten era of internal combustion here. Some machines, forklifts, shit like that. Nothing more scary than the steady stream of incoherence coming from VanMeer's head.

"Down. We have to go down, Ms. Sixa."

He breaks a beam of an electric eye, the motion swirling moats of dust. The section of the floor we're standing on begins descending.

"I'm afraid that I can't keep secrets anymore. Too much has happened." The thoughts flash through his head.

Thoughts of Riva Barnes.

"You see, I told you that what Celludyne was working on was gene therapy and micromachines to enhance and prolong human life. That was a lie, at least in contemporary terms."

"You were Riva's lover?" The question is meant to derail his trail of thought.

He nods. "You see, nothing that has to be implanted and designed for specific conditions inside the human body can be very successful for very long. The body's own structure is too wily for simplistic interventions."

"Why are you telling me this now?"

"There should be no secrets between us now. You've been used, as have I."

The floor stops abruptly The walls of the shaft begin to part.

"Anyway, with the proper financial backing, we embarked on a more ambitious project. We decided that a biological agent was necessary for the results that we wanted."

"And this is your secret lab?"

He shakes his head. "No. Not really."

The lights go on.

"We call this the autopsy machine."

It looks like a bin farm, hundreds of silvery capsules stacked in rows as far as the eye can see.

"Autopsy . . . machine. Then those are . . . bodies?"

"Part of the current crop. Let me explain. I said we thought that a biological agent was necessary, but you didn't let me explain for what." I nod, staring.

His tone is hushed, reverential. "Longevity. The key is in biogenesis, the beginnings of life on this planet. Something had to hold protoorganisms together long enough for the complex metabolic machinery of life to evolve. We began by looking at the simplest possible forms of life formed some three and a half billion years ago and began working backward from there."

We are walking through aisle and aisle of silver capsules. The tops are clear. They are all filled with dead people. Dead people with dark skin.

"Metabolism, and life itself requires isolation from the external environment. A membrane, composed of lipids and proteins. The first membranes must have been extraordinary to form under the first temperate conditions on earth as the planet cooled. They must have been capable of sustaining life before life began, by allowing only those chemicals that the first protocells found useful to penetrate the cell's inner workings."

The capsules are on a conveyor belt. As I watch a capsule is opened and a body fed to an operating theater manned solely by robots. A bone saw begins to whine and an incision is made in the body, a short black man who looks to be about thirty-five.

"Evolution required the eventual conversion of these first membranes into something less durable. It was the one discontinuity in a continuous biological process of evolution, you see, because evolution required shorter lived organisms to produce genetic change over billions of generations. The information on how to make the first membrane, utilizing what we call the universal protein, was lost."

The body is pumped out, the blood and waste products going to vials and test tubes for additional analysis. The bone saw whines again, and a circular section of the skull is neatly incised and lifted away.

"Once we were able to postulate the structure of this protein, we tested it. The results were remarkable. Prokyarotic organisms, the simplest organisms that support life, lived virtually forever when the genetic structure of their membranes was altered to include our compound. Then we began to look for ways in which we could apply those genetic alterations to higher life forms."

"What exactly are you getting at?"

"A virus. Not one that makes you sick. One that makes you well. One that incorporates a slight alteration to the protein-lipid structure of your cellular anatomy. A genetic algorithm that adapts our induced chemistry to the various cells of the body so that they are impervious to anything that can harm them but are still capable of carrying out the incredibly diverse functions of life. A hypermutable retrovirus that attaches to your cellular DNA and incorporates change."

The autopsy is complete. The next body, a black child of about ten, is swung into place on the operating table.

"The problem with a virus is that the wrong structure can just as easily kill as heal. The problem was not in developing possible agents. The problem was in testing them."

What was it VanMeer said when I first met him? *"We've been seeing viruses without natural predecessors for twenty years now."*

"And this is the result of your tests?" *Damage. They introduced versions of their virus into the general population.*

He nods. "A small portion. The end of it, really. We've been testing for two decades. Most of our first attempts were terribly virulent failures."

I bet you didn't introduce these puppies in Beverly Hills.

"But you kept testing."

"Yes. And built facilities like this one to figure out why people died."

"How many?"

VanMeer shakes his head. "We were horrified at the first results. The agents that we tested were highly infective. New diseases swept the entire world as a result of our work. Old diseases made comebacks in the wake of what happened to people's immune systems.

"But we needed the data. We thought we were working for the ultimate good of mankind."

"And Riva Barnes found out about your work."

"No. Riva knew all along what I was working on. She was my mistress."

Another capsule is manipulated into place. The capsule is opened, a standard Y type incision is made opening up the chest cavity . . .

And she was . . . part of it. Invasive measures. Viral agents. Longevity.

"People must have become suspicious."

"Invariably. Those that raised suspicions found themselves the victims of one of our failed efforts. Quite easily accomplished, I'm afraid. We could introduce a dose into your wine at a restaurant, for example, as long as we were careful about the packaging.

"Or our backers would arrange financial considerations. Or promises of the finished product. Or fatal accidents."

"And enough people could be persuaded to look the other way."

"Only a very few could put this together. The signature protein coat of a manufactured organism is quite distinctive. If you begin finding them in tissue samples from Dakar and oh, say, Jersey City, then you begin to put two and two together."

"If Riva knew, why was she killed?"

"Why was my wife killed? To make a point. To keep me on the straight and narrow. To keep these machines running until we produced the final prototype."

"Who?"

"Arnold Waters, of course."

My anger is hot and furious as I pull my gun.

"And whose idea was it to test this on poor people?"

Phillip VanMeer stops walking.

"We didn't just test it on poor people, even though that was our intent. These are infectious agents, Ms. Sixa."

"How many have died?"

VanMeer says nothing.

"HOW MANY?"

The answer appears in his head. The number is large enough to make me dizzy.

It's a reflex action. I shoot him twice.

The wheels are spinning furiously as I return to the office. I call Didi back in. Get the cappuccino machine to make me a stiff pot of the stuff. Ignore the shakes that I have, the headache. Ignore the weakness in my legs.

Nagging me at the back of my mind is the fact that I haven't called LAPD to report VanMeer's murder.

Genevive Wilkerson.

Marie Folcoup.

Riva Barnes.

The idea forms slowly at first, suppressed by the mountains of other evidence. And yet, the more I think about it, the more the solution becomes clear. It's all right there in my construction paper and circles, the overlaps, the outliers, the explanations. In the end Didi has to check out four rather simple facts in order for me to confirm my suspicions.

At dawn the answers come back. I've narrowed the field of possibilities from the limitless to the finite, a ring of concentric circles that lead to a circle of one. I've found him.

I've found Mr. Right.

The morning is a hot and sweaty one on the streets of LA. Leaving the office I take a single briefcase whose contents will help me finish the case.

I leave my gun with Didi.

I get into a cab, tell the driver the address, then tell him to take the long way so that Mr. Right will have enough time to get there. He'll be waiting, of course. He will want to be there.

Sometime later the cab deposits me at a building. I tell the doorman my name, and he rings up to check. Seconds later he lets me pass. Just like I knew he would. The elevator door opens soundless onto a long corridor lit by lights and brightened by sunlight washing through the lone window at the far end. My long walk down the marbled floors, each step like a gunshot as the terror builds because something else is behind one of these apartment doors, something more than a killer, something more than an answer.

Mr. Right is not a serial killer after all, not in the usual sense. The other victims were tied together by a common thread, a thread that wasn't obvious until Celludyne became the center of the circle.

Marie Folcoup. Genevive Wilkerson. Folcoup, daughter of a minor industrialist that did business with Celludyne by supplying specialty amino acids.

Wilkerson dated a vice president of a subcontractor that supplied microvascular pumps to a major contractor for Celludyne.

Riva Barnes. VanMeer's mistress.

Mr. Right desperate for a cure. Desperate enough to kill. I understand the desperation because I too am desperate. *Desperate enough to lie.*

Gunshot steps from my high heels. Desperation in my steps, fear in my mind.

Stop. The door is open. I close my eyes and let the wave of thoughts wash over me—

<Jenny.>

How desperate are you, Jenny?

Do you want to live forever?

<Come in, Jenny. Come in.>

In or out, Jen? In or out? You won't be able to turn back. No matter what you learn. No matter what.

One small step over the threshold onto the carpeted floor.

There's something incredibly fatalistic about running away.

The door to the apartment is open. I walk in, lay the briefcase on the sofa. From the kitchen he begins to talk:

"What finally convinced you it was me?"

I have no reason for guile.

"The first two victims. I found the connection."

"What else?"

"You had unprotected sex with Riva Barnes before you killed her. That means you already had VanMeer's magic bullet and could care less about disease."

"Very good. I trust that Mr. VanMeer is no longer with us?"

"That's correct."

He comes out of the kitchen smiling. "Was that it?"

"Not really. The night Jacqueline VanMeer was killed one of your choppers filed a flight plan that brought you back here." He is coming toward me now.

Quickly now. "No one has seen Arnold Waters since the explosion."

"Yes, Arnold. Incredibly troubling for a normal."

"You knew my gun wasn't loaded the night you killed Trainor."

He is amused.

I am not. "Why?"

He looks at me and does not answer. But I have to know—

"Why me?"

Richard Waters shakes his head. His thoughts are a thunderbolt—

<you know why, Jenny>

My last thought before Richard overwhelms me is of his hologram waving to me from the top floor of the darkened office building, just before the blast charred his father's body beyond recognition.

Stormy weather:

officer bob white looks me in the eye the day after as the wind whips the blanket covering the body. He asks me "you're a smart girl, aren't you, Jenny? You didn't have anything to do with this, did you?" and when I go to look, he forces my head away, and the tears begin, the black cop with an accurate imagination, the white teenage girl who doesn't want to remember

the bad thing
<wanna do her. wanna do her bad>

Kyle and I on the beach after the fun house, after the funny voices in my head at the house of mirrors. It's weird, because I can hear what he's going to say before he says it, I can hear the plotting in his mind.

near the boardwalk he drags me down in the sand <hit me baby you can't hurt me> *begins pulling off my clothes over my protests, shushes me with a hand over pulls down his pants, his underwear, black night overhead, no digitized illusion of clear weather here, just the eternal flame from the blown well, the black cloud drifts over us and I can't see his face*

but i feel his cock, trying to go inside me

shit It Hurts

IT HURTS! something dark like a thunderclap leaps from my mind

smashes the side of his face
—Darkness, like a thunderclap without sound pressure
a world of compression—

From my mind to his consciousness, snuffed out by the pressure . . .

Kyle is lifted off me, his eyes already rolling back into his head,

no voices now motherfucker,

nothing . . .

nothing . . .

bob white that day after;

"how'd you kill him girl? spontaneous trauma, no visible sign of death,

nothing . . ." bob white's voice a desperate whisper . . .

"don't cry Jenny, don't say anything, just leave, just leave, no proof, nothing . . ."

and I see Kyle's body, naked and barefoot under the sheet, the hair blowing gently in the ocean breeze

and I can't handle it, the bad thing repressed. The voices in my head, repressed.

<*you have done a bad thing, jenny girl. a BAD THING . . .*>

Richard had to know, oh, God, no. He saw the voices, the bad thing, the guilt leaking from beneath the barriers. The terrible knowledge of dark thunderclaps that kill without leaving signs . . .

"You knew." Reeling.

"I still love you, Jenny. Couldn't help loving you. I knew you were special. Knew I had to save your life and my own, for that matter. Didn't know if you would ever accept me or not."

He holds out a vial of capsules. VanMeer's miracle virus.

". . . but you must have this. Whether you take me in or not."

And he's right. I must have the cure.

And what if Prince Charming is a murderer?

I've been alone all my life.

He learned to kill from the memory he tore from my brain.

Isn't this my fault? Ada. Kyle. *The blanket ripples on the sand. Riva Barnes, Marie Folcoup, Genevive Wilkerson, Jacqueline VanMeer.*

The cure.

. . . and I look into his eyes and see the love first, the emotion itself sensuous/strong enough to have pushed him over the edge to murder, a shy little boy fixated on the beautiful woman that he could never imagine himself having, the beautiful woman teaching him something from her repressed memory . . .

It makes me ill. But this is who I am; Richard's depravity speaks to my destiny.

Telephone records of Genevive Wilkerson and Marie Folcoup came back ***Access Interdicted*** some fifty times when Didi tried to match them to a reverse directory. The people at the other ends of those phone numbers were somehow connected to Waters Industries.

Richard used attractive women for industrial espionage on his partners. He saved Riva for VanMeer because of the importance of the project and Riva's kinky predisposition to telepaths via her brother. The niggling fact about my gun being empty just before Trainor was killed had always been there, but Richard's supposed "death" had effectively squashed that one.

I'd heard the chopper overhead on my way to Richard's the night VanMeer's wife was killed. The pilot was conveniently unavailable, but it doesn't require rocket science to figure out a pickup point that got him out of VanMeer's home. And of course he had Erasmus Trainor for the other murders, and a general assist.

Arnold Waters the father in fear of the son's power, a useful facade for the VanMeers of the world, useful until the cure.

Richard is holding up a sealed package. The keys to immortality to be ingested with a glass of water. The virus will prevent PrP from attacking my mind as it has protected Richard's.

God help me, I need the cure.

Which do you fear most, Jenny? The madman?

I show him the contents of my briefcase. "Make me your partner," I say. *Or death?*

My lover-to-be smiles. Holds up a finger. Wait one. He does something at a console, pulls me close, scans my prints and my retinas.

"There. You have access to it all." He motions to the black velour-covered slipcase. "Shall we?"

We shall; a whisper to myself, a tremor in my soul. He continues:

"Ten years ago I knew that time was running out. I knew about the disease. I scoured the globe searching for someone doing VanMeer's work, only to find that he was here, right in my backyard."

"So you bought up interests in all of VanMeer's partners. Using, among others, Genevive Wilkerson and Marie Folcoup to get intelligence on their activities. Their weak points."

"I was desperate, Jenny. What good would all of this be if I were incapacitated? How could I have saved your life?"

I shake my head. Hearing it, confirming what I know, is just too fantastic to be believed.

"Jenny." He takes my hand, clasps it warmly. "When we traveled together I knew that I'd done the right thing. I knew that you were the one person that I could be with. You felt it, too, Jenny, I know you did."

Yes, I felt it. Damage necessitated by loveless men

circling the globe in business jets. Brilliant men. Brilliant men like VanMeer.

And now there is but one decision to be made. I take VanMeer's miracle bug and a glass of water and walk slowly to the window. The vistas are impressive if smogged over and a smudge of greasy black smoke marks the continuing insurrection in South Centro. Four pulls on my personal trigger.

Tear open the packet. Wealth and immortality awaits. Wealth like Heaven, with its digitized illusion of sunny weather far above the dead zone where normals live and die, life and death in the clouds measured in inches, in seconds, reflected in the cold soul of a bank debit, as if the money and power can make a difference to a damaged soul.

I empty the packet in my mouth and wash it down with a drink of water.

"Are you ready?" Richard asks, the black velour case containing the neural interface in his hands. His eyes are glittering, his thoughts charged to full capacitance. Love or death, I don't think it matters much to him now. There is no way to avoid this, no way to take him on, not like he is now . . .

I remove the device. The interface to my demons. The way to my heart.

I nod.

Kiss him. The leads attached to each of our heads, the tenderness of his touch, his touch about to become . . .

. . . *entry* . . . a big rush filling me, warming me, the jolt of his mind inside of mine pushing things aside to make room. His essence suffuses with mine, a silky glow from within, completion at long last.

His body slumps against me, empty of all but the

basic functions necessary to keep him alive. It is a struggle because he is a dense body mass, but I lay him on the carpet—

just about the place that Riva fell . . .

"Ready, lover?" I say aloud. His answer is a white-hot rush in my loins, all the more liquid because it comes from within. Three clicks as the hammer falls on an empty chamber, finger tightens for the last time . . .

My movements are practiced, fluid. I snatch the ugly black beetlelike device from the briefcase. I place the neural disrupter against his neck and depress the stud. The charge sends megavolts into his wonderful brain, shorting out neurons, fusing others into grey toast. The body convulses, jerks upright, then quivers as the end comes with a foul rush of bodily fluids.

The signal is prearranged, triggered by the disrupter. The doors bang down, splintered, and the police charge in with their stupid guns to see me sitting quietly with my lover, the instrument of his destruction grasped tightly in my hand.

Derrick stands over me. "So it was him all the time?" He looks sad.

"Yes." I stand up on uncertain legs.

"How did you know?"

I hand him the three entitlements cards. "I knew." Derrick looks at me, building up the courage for more rejection.

"Hmm. Well." He's looking at his feet, lovesick. I grasp the torn packet from where I'd discarded it. Move toward the kitchen and the garbage disposal. I think of

Phillip VanMeer gutshot, bleeding, and filled with muscle tranks as I loaded him into one of his capsules . . .

"Jenny?" . . . and I imagine his eyes saucer wide as the bone saw begins to whine, as the machinery of his crime eviscerates all evidence of mine.

"Jen." Trent's voice is a desperate whisper that I don't care to hear. Only Richard, locked inside of me—

Why?

and my response

<I did it for you. I did it for us.>

as VanMeer's virus begins to work. As I begin to shudder from what I've done.

Richard's engrams will die eventually, his thoughts will fade from my mind, his rage will fade, and his body is already dead. I dread those days or hours that he will be with me, desperate penance with my lover.

"Jenny?" Derrick Trent holds out a vial of Sytogene, purchased because he snooped in Nicholson's files, now made superfluous because of VanMeer's cure.

"You're leaving me now." Derrick Trent looks into the storm in my eyes and seems lost.

<oh, yeah, derrick. we're leaving you>

—and Richard makes my blood run cold as I step over his body and out into the hot breath of the city.

ABOUT THE AUTHOR

Eric James Fullilove is a CPA, an MIT graduate, and a former finance manager at CBS. He was also chief operating officer of a not-for-profit corporation that provides housing and services for homeless persons with HIV and AIDS. He lives in New Jersey where he is at work on his next novel.